W9-CJL-113

X
berts, Les.
e scent of spiced
oranges and other $ 25.95
stories

The Scent of
Spiced Oranges
and Other Stories

Other Five Star Titles
by Les Roberts:

The Chinese Fire Drill

The Scent of
Spiced Oranges
and Other Stories

Les Roberts

Five Star • Waterville, Maine

Copyright © 2002 by Les Roberts
Foreword copyright © 2002 by Les Roberts

All stories reprinted by permission of the author.
Additional copyright information on page 200.

All rights reserved.

This collection is a work of fiction. Names, characters, places
and incidents are either the product of the author's imagination,
or, if real, used fictitiously.

Five Star First Edition Mystery Series.
First Printing.

Published in 2002 in conjunction with Tekno Books and Ed
Gorman.

Set in 11 pt. Plantin by Christina S. Huff.

Printed in the United States on permanent paper.

Library of Congress Cataloging-in-Publication Data

Roberts, Les.
      The scent of spiced oranges and other stories / Les Roberts.
         p.   cm.—(Five Star first edition mystery series)
      Contents: Little cat feet—Good boys—Angel of death—The
      scent of spiced oranges—The fat stamp—The pig man—The
      catnap—The brave little costume designer—Willing to
      work—
      The gathering of the Klan.
      ISBN 0-7862-4331-7 (hc : alk. paper)
      1. Detective and mystery stories, American.   I. Title.
      II. Series.
   PS3568.O23894 S38 2002
      8133'.54—dc212   2002029965

For
Reuban and Dorothy Silver,
who set the bar of
artistic excellence
so gloriously high

Table of Contents

Foreword

It has been said that the most difficult task to perform well in the entire sporting world is to hit a baseball hurtling toward you at more than ninety miles an hour with a round stick. This truth is borne out by the astonishing statistic that even the best batsmen fail about seven times in every ten tries.

In my opinion, the most difficult task to perform well in all of literature is to craft a really good short story. And yes, probably all but the greatest writers fail seven times out of ten.

Both baseball and short story writing *look* easy—until you try to do them well.

For a novelist, the short story discipline is even more difficult to master. He or she has but ten or fifteen thousand words to work with instead of the accustomed ninety thousand. There is no time to dawdle, to describe every leaf on every tree. There are not four hundred pages of text in which to develop the characters or the settings—instead it must be accomplished by the use of short, vivid strokes of color.

Writing short stories is the best way I know of for a writer to learn to write.

In *The Arabian Nights*, Scheherezade had to stretch out her tales for a thousand and one nights just to keep her head; a short story writer does just the opposite, telling the story concisely, sharply, getting to the point as quickly as possible. John O'Hara, Dorothy Parker, Ernest Hemingway, Shirley

Jackson, Scott Fitzgerald and John Steinbeck were masters of the craft; I am in awe of what they accomplished even while writing the longer form that established them as the American literary masters of the 20th century.

Most of the stories in this collection were written by invitation. An editor was putting together an anthology, usually with a specific theme, and asked me to contribute. That meant I was not divinely inspired in the middle of the night, as I often am when I come up with an idea for a full-length novel, but have to sit down and cogitate on how I could work cats, or private eyes, or fairy tales into a terse, punchy short story. The results sometimes surprised even me.

In putting together this volume, I revisited stories that had been completed sometimes ten or more years earlier. It was an amazing journey for me, because it made me realize how much the world has changed in only a few short years. There are things in these stories that I probably would handle differently had I been writing them now. Attitudes and observations that might be perceived in this new millennium as "politically incorrect." I truly believe that political correctness is the most dangerous threat to art and creativity that exists today, and so I offer no apology for these attitudes. Every creative work, be it literature, art, film, or music, is of its own time and must be viewed as such. Viewed from today's perspective, Ernest Hemingway was an insensitive, posturing author who wrote pure testosterone-laced prose that is now probably offensive to many. But oh, the divine way in which he wrote it!

Looking back on earlier work was a revelation to me in another way as well. Every writer has the compulsion to fiddle around, to edit, to rewrite, to make tiny changes in already-existing works. There were many places that made me cringe, that I longed to *fix*. Rookie mistakes, some of them. A sentence that I liked the first time that now seemed clumsy, or a phrase I longed to replace with a better one, or a word that was echoed and should have been changed.

In the name of honesty I refrained from making any alterations to the originals. In this entire volume, I only changed three commas and one word. The stories must stand or fall as written.

This was my first published short story in almost 30 years. When Ed Gorman called and asked me to contribute to the first Cat Crimes *anthology, I wasn't sure I could pull it off. The "cat mystery" is hardly my favorite genre.*

Don't get me wrong, I'm not a cat-hater. I have a cat, who is my best friend and my muse. His name is Sonny, christened by my son Darren after the tough-guy Corleone brother in The Godfather, *and as I type these words he is sitting on my mouse pad. He's never more than six feet away from me except when he takes his afternoon nap, and I could probably write another 50,000 words a year if I didn't have to work around him.*

It's also the first appearance of my erstwhile Los Angeles actor/detective, Saxon, in short-story form. I stopped writing the Saxon novels at six, mainly because the Milan Jacovich books sell much better, but I miss the old rascal, and it's fun to revisit his world, even in a short story.

It has been pointed out to me that in all my writings about Saxon I generally savage Los Angeles. I have to plead guilty to that. I lived there for twenty-four years, working in the film and television business, and never even got a whiff of a sense of community. It's why I moved to Cleveland.

As I read the story for the first time in nine years, I realize there are resonances of Billy Wilder's classic film, Sunset Boulevard. *They were purely unintentional; I guess when an artist sees something that brilliant, it stays with him and exerts even a subliminal influence.*

The title of the story, of course, comes from Carl Sandburg's poem, "Fog," which he describes as coming on little cat feet. Little did I know that when I moved from Los Angeles to Cleveland I would become close friends with Sandburg's daughter, Helga Sandburg Crile, who lives just a few blocks from me. I'd like to think that her father would have enjoyed this story.

Little Cat Feet

The first thing I noticed was the smell. You'd have noticed it too, unless you're one of those people who cuts off your nose to spite your face.

It was an acrid, ammonia odor that made my eyes water; I could feel it sinking into my clothes and hair, the kind of stink that makes door-to-door political canvassers and magazine salesmen and Jehovah's Witnesses do a direct about-face and go away before they ever ring the doorbell. I sneezed. It was the smell of a cat litter box that hadn't received enough attention—magnified to the tenth power.

The house was a Moorish wet dream, all inlaid mosaic tiles and squinches and horseshoe arches, with jacaranda and fever trees and hummingbird enticing bottle brush growing in profusion up to the carved wooden door set into the wall around the house. It was set high in the sere hills above Cahuenga Boulevard and the Hollywood Bowl, in a neighborhood where all the eccentric has-beens from moviedom's Golden Age are holed up waiting for the bean counters who now run the industry to once again start doing films like Mr. DeMille used to make. Only an eccentric would choose to live in a house only accessible to mountain goats or four-wheel-drive vehicles, solely for the privilege of having a high-angle view of a city so socked-in by brown air pollution that it makes you cough just to look at it. They all like to go out on their balconies at night, shake their fists at the lights behind the smog, and vow, "Big town, I'll lick you yet."

I pushed the button inset into the stucco arch, and immediately got an answering buzz. As I'd been instructed, I opened the wooden door and went through into a walled garden where several varieties of palm and exotic shrubbery imported to Southern California from someplace else grew in overprofusion. The place was badly in need of pruning shears—or a machete. The door to the house was open and Louise Manaster stood framed in the archway. She was dressed in billowy crepe lounging pajamas in a rich shade of gray, and her hair was pulled back into a matching turban. Unlike many Hollywood women of her generation, she didn't resort to makeup by the trowelful, and if she'd had any cosmetic surgery it was the good kind that didn't show. I knew from my movie history that she had to be around seventy years old. She looked fifty-five, and though she was not beautiful, she was handsome instead, conveying the illusion of beauty. And in this town, the illusion is all that matters.

"Mr. Saxon?" she said. "Please come in."

The litter box smell was stronger inside the house, almost overwhelming. In the air everywhere were fine little cat hairs, and a ray of sun coming in through one of the arched windows turned them silver, dancing on a current of air. From where I stood in the atrium entry I could see eight cats in various stages of recline and repose—three Siamese, two Persian, and three shorthairs whose ancestry could probably be traced back four generations in the last year alone. One of the Siamese, a blue point, came over to me and muttered, her tail a vertical question mark over her back. I sneezed violently. I have a slight allergy to cat hair.

If you've ever seen a movie produced in Hollywood before 1962 you've seen Louise Manaster's costumes on the bodies of every leading actress in the business. Back when people knew the stars as well as their own families and the only director they knew about was Hitchcock, most Americans could have told you her name and what she did for a living. On the mantle in her living room were a row of her Academy Award statuettes, more than anyone else in film history, displayed as casually as a stonemason from Jersey might show off his bowling league trophies.

She led me into the living room and indicated that I should sit on an ornate Chinese-red sofa that curved around in an L-shape for about fourteen feet. It was covered with cat hair. Louise Manaster arranged herself on a low-slung silk pouffe that was as big as a poker table, hands clasped around one silk-clad knee. One of the cats, a gray, jumped up on my lap and began kneading my thigh with her needle claws. I gently pushed her onto the floor with the back of my hand, and sneezed three times.

"Don't you like cats, Mr. Saxon?"

"Yes, but not when I'm wearing a dark suit. And their hair gets into my nose. I guess I prefer dogs."

"Pity," she said. "Dogs are subservient, fickle, fawning, and co-dependent, and will lick the hand of whoever feeds them. But a relationship with a cat cannot be taken for granted. It must be carefully negotiated on both sides." She drew herself up proudly. "I am a cat person," she said, which told me I was in for a negotiation.

"What did you want to see me about, Miss Manaster?"

The frail shoulders rose and fell. "Do you investigate theft?"

I shrugged, not wanting to commit myself. I've been in Hollywood long enough to know that. "What's been stolen?"

She uncoiled herself from where she'd been sitting and went over to the fireplace. She was a tall woman, slim and elegant, and only her hands, liver-spotted and with enlarged knuckles, tattled on her age. She took something from the mantle where it had been hidden between two of her Oscars and brought it to me, holding it in the palm of a hand that trembled slightly. It was a jeweled pin, black onyx in the shape of a sleek cat in motion. The eyes were two emeralds, the collar was made up of tiny rubies, and there were enough diamonds in the backing to purchase a small yacht.

"This," she said. Two more cats wandered in from another part of the house. That made ten, and still counting.

Her lip curled into an unpleasant sneer. "It's obviously a copy, Mr. Saxon." It wasn't all that obvious to me. "The original was given to me by the head of a major studio many years ago, as a sort of thank-you gift. I discovered it missing the same night Derek left me."

"Derek?" She was going to tell it in her own way, I could see that, and in her own sweet time. I leaned back on the hairy sofa, ready to dig in for the duration.

Derek Hawke had come to town eight months earlier from someplace in the midwest where they grow corn and mine gypsum, determined to hit it big in films or television. You've heard the story before; we all have. He was a big hunky guy with blue eyes and golden hair, and had gotten a job as a stock boy at the May Company on Wilshire Boulevard and Fairfax Avenue, where after only two days he was "discovered" by Louise Manaster. She'd installed him in her Moorish palace in the hills and footed the bill for a new wardrobe, acting lessons, and a leased Cadillac convertible, and had made a few calls to old friends who were still alive and hanging on at the studios. She didn't have as much influence in town as the bus boy at Spago's—she hadn't costumed a film since the early seventies and half the hairy-nosed children who now run the business never even heard of her. But poor Derek, the movie-struck kid, had heard of her, counted the Oscars over the hearth, and perceived in her a ticket to fame.

And then two nights ago, the lovebirds had quarreled—loud enough for all the neighbors to hear them—and after making a phone call Derek had stomped out, taking with him only a small overnight bag.

"What was the argument about?" I said.

She waved a vague hand. "He felt his career wasn't progressing as it should have. I tried to explain that some things take time, but . . ." She sat down again, playing with the pin, rubbing it between thumb and forefinger like a lucky penny.

It's amazing how many innocents of both genders come from the provinces and drop their drawers in this town for a chance at stardom, and how few of them actually sleep with the right people.

"Why didn't he take his convertible?" I interrupted.

She looked sad, ruined. "He threw the keys at me. He said he didn't want anything of mine. That's why he left all his clothes here."

I was impressed. A gigolo with scruples. Every day brings something new, I suppose.

"He called me—oh, he said some terrible things to me, Mr. Saxon. I don't think I can ever forgive him for that." She covered her face with her hands.

I put my knuckle up under my nose to stifle another cat-induced sneeze. "And you think he stole the real pin?"

"Certainly not!" she said.

I held my hands out, palms up. "Then . . . ?"

"It was a mistake, a—an impulsive misjudgment, that's all. Derek is no thief. The pin was out on the coffee table—I'd just reclaimed it from the jeweler, who'd replaced a loose clasp. I think he just—took it by accident."

Sure. And Santa Claus, the Tooth Fairy, and the Easter

Bunny were all paid-up members of the Screen Actor's Guild.

The story stunk. It had a lousy beat, you couldn't dance to it, and I gave it about a fifty-five. "What is it you want me to do?"

"Get my pin back," Louise Manaster said.

Cute. She was figuring if I found the pin I'd find her precious Derek. Maybe I would.

I could have just said no. That would have been the smart thing. But I'm an old movie buff, too. How could I refuse the woman who had dressed Lana Turner, Ava Gardner, Katharine Hepburn, Lauren Bacall and Rita Hayworth? Besides, this way I could bill her for having the cat hair cleaned out of my suit.

Otherwise I'd be sneezing for a month.

The first thing I did was to check the sleazy hockshops down on South Main Street, and on Sherman Way in the San Fernando Valley, but I did so with small faith. The pin was probably in the pocket of some junkie trying to unload it in a parking lot along with ten or twelve watches he'd wear all up and down both arms. There must be at least ten thousand down-and-outers to fit that description in L.A.

Louise Manaster had given me a list of names she'd called on Derek's behalf, people she knew in the industry. They obviously hadn't gotten him a contract, but other than the guys in the stockroom at the May Company, all of whom were themselves stars of tomorrow, I couldn't think of anyone else in town who knew him.

Albert Sussman wasn't one of the original founders of Monarch Pictures, but he'd been there since the beginning and produced several films which you've probably seen on a cable station specializing in oldies. Now in his eighties, he maintained an office on the lot, the old-timers from the prop department or studio security tipped their hats to him and called him Mr. Sussman, and everyone else pretty much ignored him. There were high-level executives at Monarch, guys in their late thirties or early forties who oversaw every phase of the filmmaking operation, who hadn't the foggiest idea who Sussman was, and were just waiting for him to die so they could utilize his office.

"Ah, one of Louise's protégés," he said, nodding. "They come and go so quickly, it's hard to keep track. It's a damn shame, a woman like that, at her age, running around with some young putz the age of her grandchildren . . ."

"Don't you go out with women young enough to be your grandchildren, Mr. Sussman?"

He switched his cigar from the left corner of his mouth to the right. "I don't 'go out' with them. They're hookers. It's an entirely different proposition."

"Could you take a look at this for me?" I said, showing him a headshot I'd found in Derek Hawke's personal effects. In fact I'd found about five hundred in all, a not-yet-arrived actor's calling card. He looked handsome, vulnerable, and nearly indistinguishable from all the other kids his age who were waiting on tables or working in stockrooms or had latched on to some rich and ultimately powerless patron like Louise Manaster.

Sussman studied it. "This one, yes. He was in here about a month ago, wanting to be a star. I didn't see much magic in him, Mr. Saxon. There's a million pretty faces and bodies out there—youth is a commodity that's a drug on the market—but there has to be magic or else it's no good. James Dean. The young Brando. Cagney, Gary Cooper, Jimmy Stewart—that kind of magic. This kid?" He smacked his lips around the cigar and gave a deprecating little wave. "I made a few calls for him, but nobody much listens to me anymore around here, so it came to nothing." He shook his head sadly. "He seemed to know he was on a treadmill. There was a sadness about him." He raised his eyebrows. "Not that good, bankable Montgomery Clift kind of sensitivity, mind you. Just a sad kid."

"Sad about what?"

"What did he have to be glad about?" Sussman said. "No talent, no career, not a pot of his own to piss in, and screwing a woman fifty years his senior just to survive. Of course he was a sad kid!" He pushed the picture back across the desk at me as though it were grossly pornographic. "I give him one more month in this town before it chews him up and spits him out."

"Sad, Mr. Sussman—do you mean desperate, too?"

"You go beyond that here," he said. "You realize that your whole life you've been chasing the wind, you don't get desperate. You get down—lower down than a worm's ass—once you realize you aren't worth two cents in a town that loves a buck the way a nun loves her beads."

"Is that where Derek Hawke was when you saw him?"

He carefully, deliberately blew smoke at me. Most of the time I gag on cigar smoke, but this cigar was so fine and so expensive that I didn't mind it. I rather liked it, in fact.

"Close," he said.

The Bolt-Sharman Agency was located south of Wilshire on Beverly Drive, in one of those two-story low-rent office buildings that survive only because there's not enough room to build a high-ticket glass monolith in its place. The building had been there for forty years, and so had Frank Sharman, whose heyday had coincided with those low-budget *Attack of the Giant Puppet People* features of the middle fifties. Then Irving Bolt died, and the agency, now on hard times, handled day players—pretty young people who could stand around looking good and not have to act, who might pick up a few days' work a month but would never see their name above the title. If they had anything on the ball they left Frank Sharman early in their careers; in fact, it was well known in casting circles that if Bolt-Sharman represented you, you were pretty much a loser.

"Derek Hawke? Yeah, I sent him out on a couple of calls," Frank Sharman said. He was seventy-two years old, and affected the rich hippie look of the late, lamented Love Generation—long sideburns, a vivid silk shirt, faded blue jeans, and a scarf. His glasses were steel-rimmed, perfectly round, and the lenses were tinted gray. All that was missing was a Liverpudlian accent and Yoko Ono hanging on his arm.

"I only bothered with him as a favor to Louise. It's not enough to look nice—the kid just doesn't have any pizzazz. I knew it when he walked in the door. I'm surprised Louise didn't know it, either." He smiled and gave us one of those just-between-us-guys leers. "Of course her judgment was— ah—clouded." He made a circle of his left thumb and forefinger and made an in-and-out motion through it with his right middle finger. Just in case I hadn't gotten his drift. Just in case I was terminally stupid.

"You have an address for him?"

He pursed his mouth. "Louise's house."

"Do you know his friends, then? Who he hung out with?"

"Hung out?" Sharman sat forward in his chair. "He hung out here. In my waiting room. Every goddamn day, whining for a job, for an audition, for some crumb." He shook his head. "All actors are crybabies, but they ought to frame him."

All of a sudden he remembered who he was talking to, but he was discomfited only a little bit. "Sorry. I forgot you're in the business, too. But I've been an agent for forty years and I can spot a winner coming down the street—or a loser. You know what I mean?"

"Yeah, I know what you mean," I said. I hate movie people—they're all very impressed with themselves. In my hunt for Louise Manaster's cat pin I was running into a lot of them. "Do you remember what calls you sent him out on?"

"That was six weeks ago," he said. "I don't even remember if my bowels moved this morning. Ask Paige."

"Paige?"

He waved his hand toward the door. "The girl."

Frank Sharman's "girl" was a fresh-faced kid of about twenty-three, with honey-colored hair and a complexion right out of Iowa. Periwinkle-blue eyes. The body of a cheerleader. The nameplate on her desk said she was Paige Smith. Smith, for God's sake. She'd probably been a straight-B student, was voted Best Personality by her senior class, and made Toll House cookies that'd knock your socks off. You know the type. I wanted to ask what a nice girl like her was doing in a place like Hollywood. But I knew. The same thing they're all doing here—chasing after empty dreams and trying to convince themselves they're living.

The entire city of Los Angeles is in denial.

She was going through her casting sheets, her tongue sticking out between her teeth as she concentrated, running down the list of names with a pink-tipped fingernail that was too long for a secretary but just right for an aspiring movie queen. I noticed the finger trembled a bit, and that there were purplish smudges beneath those blue eyes. Hollywood was giving her a rough time, I supposed. What a surprise. I wondered if it was drugs, booze, or a shattered love affair. Or maybe just that she'd come out here to be a star, like Derek Hawke, and had suddenly opened her eyes to find herself someone's "girl" at a fly-by-night agency that couldn't have gotten Olivier a job if they were doing *Hamlet* down on the corner.

"We sent Derek Hawke over to ABC for extra work on a soap on the seventeenth of June," she said. "And to Disney— well, Touchstone—about a picture on the twenty-fifth." Her voice sounded soft and muffled, like she'd just drunk a glass of milk.

"Did he get either one of them?"

She shook her head sadly. "Not even a callback. Look, he isn't in any trouble, is he?"

"I don't know. Why?"

Her shrug was elaborately offhanded. "He just seemed like a nice guy, that's all. He was over here a lot, and I sort of got to know him."

"I don't suppose you'd know where he might be."

She stared at something absolutely fascinating about four inches above my head. "I didn't know him *that* well."

"Oh."

"Sometimes when people come in here you get involved with their problems whether you want to or not. You know, they sit around waiting for something to come in so they can go out on a call, and you get to talking . . ."

"Uh-huh."

"It's no big deal."

"No," I said, and pointed at the casting ledger. "Anything else?"

She resumed her search, and when she spoke again her voice was lower, less shrill. "Here—he went to read for Andrew Nicholson on the third."

"June third?"

"Uh-huh."

I jotted Nicholson's name down on my little Spiral pad.

"Do you remember the last time you saw Derek?"

"Last Monday," she said promptly. The day he disappeared from Louise Manaster's bed and board. With the cat pin.

I gave her my business card. "It's kind of important that I find him. Will you call me if you see him again?"

"I probably won't see him again."

"I thought he hung out here a lot."

"Oh well, yes, but if he's in some sort of trouble . . ."

She didn't finish her sentence. She didn't have to.

At about eight o'clock the next morning a Korean gardener discovered Derek Hawke's body. He was down at the foot of Louise Manaster's hill, just off the edge of her property line, staring at the smog-stained sky with sightless eyes. There were stab and slash wounds in his neck, stomach, and finally in his chest. A subsequent coroner's report said that he had been dead since Monday evening, and that the cause of death seemed to be from a pointed-dull-edged instrument like a nail file. Wherever he'd been heading when he slammed out of Louise Manaster's house, he hadn't gotten very far.

I heard the news on the radio, and immediately checked with Lieutenant Joe DiMattia of LAPD Homicide, who told me the only belongings they'd found on or near the body were an overnight bag with underwear and socks, a shaving kit, a wallet with a driver's license from the state of Missouri, and forty-six dollars and change in his pocket. No cat pin. Maybe the Korean gardener had swiped it before he called the cops—but I didn't think so.

It was DiMattia's personal opinion that the Manaster woman had killed Derek Hawke because he was trying to leave her, and all my protestations that she would have hardly dumped him down the hill and left him there for two days fell on deaf ears. Maybe it was because she was my client and he wanted to believe the worst of her. Maybe he really thought his scenario made sense. Joe *DiMattia* could be the poster boy for that slogan about a mind being a terrible thing to waste.

When I got to the house, a grave-looking older man in a vest, tie and shirtsleeves opened the door, announced that he was Miss Manaster's doctor, and said she couldn't see anyone right now because she was "prostrate" and under sedation.

If I had Joe DiMattia suspecting me of murder I'd be prostrate, too. She had the motive and the opportunity, but somehow she didn't strike me as the type of person who'd kill a young man and leave him down at the bottom of the hill for the mice. Or care that someone else had. Louise Manaster had been in Hollywood long enough to know that everything is temporary—careers, lovers, TV series, they all had their time and then they were no more. That's why almost ninety per cent of the buildings in town have been built since 1968.

Several cats, including one I hadn't seen before, swirled lazily around the doctor's feet like water rising in a bathtub. I said, "Please tell Miss Manaster I came by."

He looked at me with distaste. "You're a trifle older than her usual companions. You won't last, you know."

I sat in the car and smoked a cigarette before driving back down the hill. I repressed a shudder; being mistaken for Louise Manaster's fancy man wasn't my idea of a joke. How many other young men and women, coming to Hollywood to chase a dream, had fallen into the same kind of dead-end trap? I was glad I had my investigations agency to support me during the lean times. At least I could face myself in the bathroom mirror every morning.

Louise Manaster had given me a healthy retainer, which

made me feel better about the whole thing. I'm not dumb—I knew that the object of the whole exercise was not to recover her gem-encrusted cat but to recover her young lover. With him dead, it seemed rather pointless. Items like that are usually insured and can be replaced.

But I did have her money, and a contract to find the jeweled cat pin, so I doggedly kept at it. Maybe Andrew Nicholson knew something about it.

He was one of those Hollywood characters that seems to show up at every party, every charity function, every major premiere. He had produced a few low-budget pictures that no one remembered, but ask anyone in town about Andrew Nicholson and they'll either tell you about his open predilection for good-looking young boys, or the fact that he had inherited more money than he knew what to do with from his mother, who had not only been a mid-level star in the thirties, but had made several marriages to movie moguls and investment bankers that had been, to say the least, financially if not emotionally rewarding.

Nicholson's house was up above Sunset Plaza Drive in West Hollywood, with an even better view of the smog than from the Manaster place. Alabaster statues of well-endowed Greek males standing before Doric columns flanked the doorway. I don't know who it was that let me in, but he was about nineteen, with beefy shoulders and biceps and the kind of tan you have to work at, and was wearing a lavender tank top and white rayon shorts. He had violet eyes and a full, sensual mouth, and tufts of black hair stuck out from under his arms like the wings of a raven.

"Andrew is out by the pool," he said. He wasn't very happy to see me; maybe he was worried that I'd cut in on his action. Andrew Nicholson's relationships with young men tended not to last much more than a few months, and perhaps this one was sensing that his time on the hill was running out. In any case, he gracelessly left me standing in the atrium while he went off to do whatever it was he did to fill his waking hours. Probably there was an exercise room somewhere in the house that had been built just for him, or his predecessor, or twenty predecessors past.

Andrew was indeed out by the pool, which I managed to find without much trouble on the other side of a thirty-foot wall of glass. That's why they pay me the big bucks.

"Mr. Saxon, how delightful to see you again," he said, not getting up. I couldn't remember where I'd met him, and I'm sure he couldn't either, but the way he said delightful left no doubt in my mind that it wasn't.

He was stretched out on a chaise longue, wearing a skimpy black bikini and basted from head to foot with tanning oil. An expensive tape deck was playing Tchaikovsky next to his ear. He was in pretty good shape for a man of fifty, but he didn't look as though he used the exercise room the way his live-in friend did. He invited me to sit down by patting the pad next to him, but I chose a deck chair several feet away. No fool I.

"Shall I have Sean bring you something to drink?"

I politely declined and told him why I was there.

"Of course I remember Derek Hawke," he said. "A lovely young man. He read for me some weeks ago."

"For what?"

"I'm preparing to do a picture. The script is nearly finished."

I knew what that meant. Nothing. It was either the standard brand of Hollywood bullspeak to cover the fact that he had nothing going at the moment, or else Frank Sharman was sending him handsome young actors to interview just for the hell of it. There is little difference between a Hollywood agent and a pimp anyway, but most aren't quite as blatant about it.

At least pimps get to wear more interesting clothes.

"When's the last time you saw him?"

He lay back on the cushion, eyes closed, baking in the afternoon sun. "I don't really recall. Perhaps two weeks ago."

"But he read for you on June third. This is July eighteenth."

"Mmm-hmmmm," he said, his tone insinuating.

"So you saw him after the reading?"

"Of course I did. Don't be tiresome, Mr. Saxon."

I leaned over and snapped off the music. "If you'd listen to the radio instead of your tapes, Andrew, you'd know that Derek Hawke has been murdered."

His eyes flew open and beneath his tan he lost a lot of color. He sat up. "My God," he said.

"If I could trace him back here, the police can, too. So I suggest you talk to me."

"Are you implying . . . ?"

"No," I said. "I just want to talk."

He mopped his face with a fluffy red towel. In the bright sunlight I could tell he'd had extensions done in his hair. "What can I tell you about?"

"The relationship, for starters."

He smiled without mirth. "There was none."

"Hard to believe, knowing you."

He put a hand over his heart. "Scout's honor. Our friend Derek suddenly got religion. The seeds of corruption were in that young man's soul—but he finally said no more. It seems the little slut was in love with someone else and just wouldn't feel right about—making any arrangements with me."

"And you accepted that?"

The smile turned nasty. "Never let it be said that I stood in the way of the course of true love." He leaned over toward me. "I hope my name can be left out of any official inquiry. If

I'm going to be dragged through the tabloids at least I should get something out of it."

"If you're telling the truth, you shouldn't have any problem. Derek didn't happen to mention who he was in love with, did he?"

He shook his head. "Some *woman*." The way he said it made it a dirty word. Then all at once he looked at me as if he'd never seen me before. "Hmmm. I don't suppose you'd be interested in—auditioning for me?"

I looked off toward the house where the young man who'd let me in was lurking near a French door, watching us sullenly. "I don't think Sean would like it."

"The Seans of this world come and go, you know that. The Derek Hawkes, too. But someone more mature, someone that I could actually talk to . . ."

I stood up, heading for the exit. "Dare to dream," I said.

I waited outside the office until about six o'clock, unnoticed in the general Beverly Hills evening rush. Finally I saw her come out the front door of the building, looking ashen and drawn. She headed for the public parking garage down the block as though picking up each foot was an effort. I followed her up to the second level, to a white 1982 Toyota Corolla with a crumpled fender and a sagging headliner. She fumbled with her keys to open the car door.

"Hello, Paige," I said.

She jumped and screamed, her voice echoing in the parking structure. Then she saw who it was and put a hand to her chest in the valley between her breasts. "Mr. Saxon!" she giggled breathlessly. "You scared me."

"Sorry. I just wanted to talk to you some more. Away from Frank, away from the office."

"What about?" she said. It might have been skepticism I

saw on her face—a fresh, wholesome-looking kid like that walking around Beverly Hills, I'm sure a lot of guys "just wanted to talk" to her. Or it might have been something else.

"About Derek Hawke," I said.

She dropped her eyes. "Oh." She fumbled at the door lock, finally swung it open. "I heard what happened to him. That's just awful."

"Do you want to grab a cup of coffee somewhere?"

She looked at her watch and shook her head. "I don't think so. I have to get home."

"Can we just sit in the car a few minutes, then?" That seemed to frighten her so I added, "I'm relatively harmless."

She pressed her lips together, her brows knitting prettily, and she got into the car and reached over to unlock the passenger door for me. I slid in next to her over brand new sheepskin seat covers.

"Paige, how long had you and Derek been seeing each other?"

"How did you—we weren't—he was just an actor who came into the office . . ."

"He told Andrew Nicholson he was in love. It couldn't have been Louise Manaster. From the way you acted when I talked to you yesterday, I took a shot that it might be you. Both you and Derek were the same type—you could have posed for an all-American-couple-goes-to-Burger-King ad. I thought perhaps you might have—found each other out here."

She just stared, eyes wide and level.

"Am I right, Paige?"

She turned sulky, Molly Ringwald rebelling against her parents. "All right, we were seeing each other. What of it?"

"He walked out of Louise Manaster's on Monday night without the car she'd leased for him. The house is way up in the hills—I think he called you to come and pick him up." My nose began itching and I rubbed it almost violently, feeling the cartilage pop.

She didn't answer.

"He made a phone call before he left the Manaster house, and I'd be willing to bet he called you to come and get him. You hadn't known about Louise Manaster until that moment, had you? You thought you had Derek all to yourself. You didn't know you were sharing him with a seventy-year-old woman. You were in love with him, and when you found out he was a kept plaything, you got angry and stabbed him with your nail file. Right here in the front seat. That's probably why you have brand new seat-covers on a car that's ready for the junk heap."

Her face had turned several shades grayer, and the dark smudges I'd seen beneath her eyes when I first met her were back. I found myself feeling sorry for her.

"You didn't mean to kill him," I said as gently as I could. "You found out the man you thought you loved was just a notch above a male hooker, and you lost it. Struck out. You had to get down the hill from the Manaster place. You figured the police would suspect Louise, and there was no way they could connect Derek to you. Except the cat pin. Did you keep it as a memento? Expensive souvenir—about two hundred grand worth."

She fell back against the door, stricken. Her hand was at her throat and she looked to be in deep shock. Anything in the six figures does that to people.

"That was a mistake, Paige. I wasn't after Derek—I just wanted the pin. If you'd left it in his pocket, I would have dropped the whole thing."

"You can't prove anything," she said, her voice quivering like a little kid's when you tell her she has to go to sleep.

"Sure I can. Just tell the police to search your apartment for the pin. But I didn't even have to do that." I pointed down to the floor of her car at my feet. "Cat hair," I said. "From Derek's clothes? Gets me every time."

I sneezed twice and took the car keys away from her.

In August of 1992, for reasons known only to them, The Plain Dealer, *Cleveland's only daily, decided to run two short stories in their Sunday magazine, and asked me to write one.*

This story brought me closer to big trouble, and to a lawsuit, than anything else I have ever written. It involves two drug-dealing brothers, Roy and Troy, whose mother lives in a run-down old building on Cleveland's west side, on the corner of Lorain and West 103rd Street. The day after the story was published the newsroom at The Plain Dealer *received an irate phone call from a man named Roy who owned a bar on Lorain and West 103rd Street and who had a brother named Troy. He said the entire neighborhood was laughing it him, even his city councilman had dropped by to inquire as to whether he was really dealing drugs, and he was thinking about calling a lawyer.*

The fact is, I'd never heard of him OR his brother. Troy and Roy were two little boys my son played with in Los Angeles some fifteen years earlier, and I used their names in the story. The editor asked if I would please call him and try to smooth things out. When I did, he was no longer irate, and somewhat amused by my explanation. I sent him an inscribed copy of my current book, and have never heard from him again.

The character of TV news reporter Ginger Carville surfaced again in my novel, Collision Bend *and, sadly, met a tragic fate.*

Good Boys

The building, located just off Lorain Avenue on West 103rd Street in Cleveland, was probably seventy years old if it was a day, and the smells of all those years of cooking, of pierogis and corned beef and chicken soup and kielbasa, had permeated the walls and carpets like water in a sponge. The apartments had been created by cutting the upper floor, once one large living space, into four different units, but even that had been accomplished so long ago that the place emanated the scent of old age, of sorrow and desperation along with that of ten thousand suppers.

The cameraman was fiddling with his light cables, looking for an outlet to plug them into. "Dollars to donuts we blow a fuse," he said to the audio guy, who was hunkered down over his portable unit and fiddling with the dials trying to get a sound level.

"Could you talk into the microphone, please?" the audio guy said to the old woman.

She shifted uncomfortably on the rump-sprung sofa covered with a faded, threadbare flower pattern, dropped her chin down onto her bony chest and stared at the little microphone clipped to the collar of her old blue dress like a preserved scarab beetle. The audio guy could see the unhealthy gray of her scalp showing beneath her sparse white hair. "What should I say?" she said.

"Just count from one to ten."

"One," the old lady croaked, and in her head she silently added "Mississippi."

"Two . . ."

"A little faster, please?"

"Should I start over?"

The audio guy, a handsome African American from Chicago who'd majored in electronic communication at Carnegie Tech, repressed his annoyance. "That'll be fine," he said. He glanced over at the battered TV set on the card table against the wall and thought to himself that the woman had probably never watched a newscast in her life; she just sat around gobbling up old reruns of "Who's the Boss?" and watching the transsexuals on "Geraldo." In fact, sometimes he wondered if anyone ever watched the news, if what he'd chosen for a profession wasn't somehow beside the point.

On her side of it, this was the first time in her life the old woman had ever had a person of color in her home, much less telling her what to do, and she was uneasy about it. But she figured if that's what it took to get the story told the way she wanted it, she'd just do what she had to do. She resumed her counting, and when she got to seven she hesitated so that everyone was afraid she couldn't go any higher. But she swallowed and went on.

"Eight . . . nine . . . ten." She had the voice of a crow, and there was no mistaking the rural southern Ohio origins in the nasal twang of her speech.

"Very nice, Mrs. Keighley. Ginger?"

Ginger Carville, sitting on the sofa next to the old lady, covered her own microphone, turned her head away and cleared her throat. Then she dropped her hand to her lap. "Testing one, two, three . . ." She had some irritation to swallow as well; she'd asked everyone at the station to call her Virginia in keeping with the dignity of her new position as a field reporter. But she'd been with Channel 12 for three years now as Ginger, and they kept forgetting.

"Got it," the audio guy said.

The cameraman plugged the scoop light into the socket just above the yellowed baseboard, stood up and switched on the power, and it was as if the sun had suddenly floated in through the window and turned into a bright, glaring ball in the middle of the living room. The old lady shielded her watery blue eyes with her hand. "Lord!" she said. "You got to have that on?"

The cameraman went and adjusted the foil-covered reflecting screen so the glare was even hotter.

"Yes, ma'am," he said. "And you'll have to take your hand down from your face so we can see you."

Trembling, the old lady clasped both hands between her bony thighs, squinting against the painful glare, black dots dancing on her eyeballs like the notes of a Bach fugue.

Ginger Carville leaned forward and touched Mrs. Keighley's clasped hands, the knobby, swollen knuckles, the dry skin with the raised veins and liver spots on their backs, like a contour road map of Hell. "You'll get used to the light," she soothed, trying not to shudder at the contact. This was the closest Ginger had ever been to what she considered poor white trash, and she was vaguely uncomfortable. A 1989 Kent State graduate, she had worked at Channel 12 as an unpaid intern, a floor manager, and later a news writer, just waiting for her chance to get on the air. The budget cuts of George Bush's recession had trimmed some of the higher-priced news talent from the station's roster, and they were only too glad to give Ginger a shot as a field reporter while paying her almost the same salary she'd been getting as a writer. Besides, Vivian Truscott, the anchorwoman at six and eleven o'clock, had suggested and then approved her, mainly because Ginger's mousy girl-next-door prettiness was no threat to her own somewhat glacial patrician beauty.

"Let's get it," the cameraman said, hoisting his minicam onto his shoulder and looking through the eyepiece. "We'll start wide and then zoom in slowly on Mrs. Keighley."

"Okay," Ginger said, giving her hair a final pat and dabbing at her forehead with a tissue. She was sweating like a pig in the August heat, but she was wearing a lightweight blue suit with the jacket on anyway, mainly so the sweat stains under the arms of her white blouse would be hidden from the camera's eye. She arranged herself artfully on the sofa, pressing her knees together so the camera wouldn't peek up her skirt.

She'd already explained to the old woman that they'd begin the story in the studio and then cut directly to the tape they were making now, so there was no need for an intro. Her tongue flickered over her lips so they'd be glossy looking. She wanted this to be good. Up until now the news director at Channel 12 had only let her cover benefit parties and restaurant openings and maple syrup festivals in Geauga County and lightweight stories about the arts. This was the first real "hard news" assignment she'd been given, and she was determined to make it right, to prove to everyone that she wasn't a Twinkie.

As in many male-run and male-dominated industries, pretty women in the TV news business were always considered Twinkies until they could prove otherwise, and this was Ginger's big chance, the decisive moment that comes all too infrequently to everyone at least once, where the direction of one's life could be significantly altered. If this story turned out as good as she thought it would, other hard news assignments would be sure to follow, giving her more credibility with viewers—and that could even lead to a weekend or substitute anchor spot if she played her cards right. She was the only female Caucasian reporter on the staff, and though no one was going to unseat Vivian Truscott in any foreseeable future, Ginger felt she was well positioned to make an impact at the station.

"We're rolling," the cameraman said. He waited a few seconds and then announced, "We've got speed."

"Mrs. Keighley," Ginger said in her firm, no-nonsense on-the-air voice, "how long have your sons been missing?"

The old woman jumped as if someone had touched her with a cattle prod. "Huh?"

"Mrs. Keighley," Ginger said again in the same tone, knowing they'd edit out the first false start later, "how long have your sons been missing?"

"May Three. They didn' come home that night, they didn' call, nothin'. They said they was goin' out—most nights they'd go down to the Flats and drink beer and play darts. They was good dart players—s'pecially Roy. But Troy, too. Both of 'em was good at the darts." Her old voice quavered. "I miss 'em somethin' terrible. They was good boys."

"When they didn't come home that night, or the next day, why didn't you call the police?"

Mrs. Keighley looked at her scornfully, still squinting because of the light. "Police don't want no truck with poor people," she said, smacking her lips noisily over the few teeth she had left. "They wouldn'a done nothin'. 'Sides, Roy an' Troy, they both had them a prison record." She turned her gaze to the camera as if appealing to it. "That shouldn' mean that no one cares what happens to 'em. Eve'body makes mistakes."

"But you say you think you know what happened to . . ." Ginger stopped, exasperated with herself. "Wait a minute, Jeff, that stunk."

"Just keep going, babe, we'll edit," the cameraman said. "We're still rolling."

She composed herself quickly. "What do you think happened to them?" Ginger said. She was aware that the cameraman was shifting position ever so slightly, that he was zooming his lens in on a close-up of the old lady's seamed, ravaged face.

Mrs. Keighley's head bobbed like a bird's on the scrawny stem of her neck. "I b'lieve that Joseph Rubio kilt 'em. Or had 'em kilt," she said.

Ginger waited for her to go on, but she didn't. Finally Ginger said, "That's a very serious charge, Mrs. Keighley. What makes you think that?"

Mrs. Keighley waved a claw-like hand in front of her face. "I hear things," she said mysteriously. "You live in a neighborhood like this, you hear things—on the street. I ain't sayin' no more."

"What would Joseph Rubio have against your sons?"

"Rubio, he said Roy an' Troy owed him some money. Lot of money. An' when they wouldn' tell him where it was, he kilt 'em. I bet you right now they's out there somewhere at the bottom of Lake Erie." Her lip quivered and her eyes grew bright with tears. "So cold . . ." she murmured. A tremor shook her brittle old frame.

"And *did* Roy and Troy owe Joseph Rubio money?"

"They didn' know where it was, the money. I swear by Jesus they didn'." The old woman blinked and drew herself up a little straighter, catching her breath with the effort. "I'm not sayin' Roy an' Troy never made no mistakes, 'cause they did. When you're red-dirt poor, you do crazy things sometimes an' you make the mistakes. They did their time for 'em, too, they paid their debt to the law, an' the slate was clean with them. They was good boys after all. They always was kind to me. Sometimes they'd even give me a little money so's I'd have more than jus' the Social Security. "Gu'm'int cut off the welfare last year, an' a body cain' live on jus' the Social Security 'thout starvin' to death anyways. An' I need my medicine—for my heart, y'know. So Roy an' Troy, they take keer of me, showed me respect. An' you show me a boy who takes keer his momma, that's a good boy in my book." She wiped some of the spittle from her lips with the back of her hand.

"Was this drug money?" Ginger said, leaning forward a little. Her heart was thudding in her chest now that she was zeroing in for the kill. "Were Roy and Troy working for Joseph Rubio as drug runners?"

Mrs. Keighley closed her mouth tight like a mail slot in the middle of her face. Then she said, "Don' know nothin' about any of that. Jus' know he kilt my boys an' put 'em in Lake Erie." A tear trickled down her cheek, diverted by the deep lines in her face. "Bet he hurt 'em some, too, 'fore he done it." Her eyes turned inward for a moment, almost as if she'd become unaware of the microphone, the camera and the bright light, the strangers in her tiny living room. He done it before, Rubio—hurt people. He like to do it."

The audio man had one hand on his earphones, and with the other he was manipulating a knob on his console, staring at the dial. He was smiling and nodding his head.

"Your sons disappeared at the beginning of May and this is the middle of August," Ginger pressed on, knowing that now she was mining pure gold. "Why did you wait more than three months to make this accusation?"

"Skeered silly, that's why!" The frail shoulders slumped and she put one hand up to her creepy throat. "If Joseph Rubio kilt my Roy an' Troy, y' think he'd even say boo-cat about kiln' a old lady? But now they say he's in prison his own self, so he cain' get to me. Soon's I hear that, I called you folks."

"And why did you contact Channel 12 instead of the police?"

"I tol' you 'bout the police!" she said. "An' that man of your program on the TV, he says if you got a problem you cain' solve, you should to call them an' they'd fix it."

"Mrs. Keighley—how much money do you have to live on now?"

The old woman was silent for a moment, thinking, and Ginger looked up at the cameraman in alarm, but he signaled her to keep going. She waited.

Finally Mrs. Keighley said, "The Social Security comes to a hunnerd and four dollars every month." Then she added, "an seventy-two cent."

Ginger said, "So the recent welfare cuts impacted you in a negative way?"

"Huh?"

Ginger shook her head. This was not the time to make a political statement. She'd see to it that question and the response were cut out of the final tape. Her knee touched Mrs. Keighley's by accident and, repulsed, she pulled it away quickly, then glanced up to see if the camera had caught it, but the lens was pointing away from her, right at the old woman.

"What did you hope to gain by coming forward, Mrs. Keighley?"

"I jus' wanna see justice. Joseph Rubio kilt Roy an' Troy and I want him to swing for it, tha's all. They was innocent. I'm not sayin' they never done wrong things, but they never took his money—I know that."

"*How* do you know that?"

She sniffed. "Jus' do. I knowed my boys, and they tol' me

41

they didn' take his money an' I b'lieved 'em. They never lied to they momma. They was good boys."

The tears were flowing freely now and the woman's loose mouth was shaking with her effort to contain them.

The cameraman said, "Would you say that again please, ma'am?"

"What?"

"They were good boys."

He moved closer to Mrs. Keighley and Ginger just knew that he was on what they called an ECU—an extreme close-up, the sorrowing, lined face wet with tears filling up the frame.

"Roy an' Troy, they was good boys," the old lady said again dutifully.

"I think that's got it, Jeff," Ginger said.

"OK, good," the cameraman replied. "Ma'am, if you'd stay right where you are for a second so I can do some cutaways?"

"What?"

"Just stay right there and kind of cheat a little bit toward Ginger."

"Cheat?"

"Just turn your body a little bit." He walked over, the camera still rolling, and moved her shoulder with his hand. The bones were sharp and brittle, just beneath the skin.

"Okay, Ginger, you're listening to her."

He edged his way over to the end of the sofa behind the old woman, shooting over her left shoulder, the fuzzy gray curls just peeking into the side of the frame, and focused on Ginger nodding her head as if she was agreeing, then shaking it sadly at the injustice of it all. A look of infinite, almost Madonna-like pity drew a vertical line between her carefully shaped eyebrows. "Mm-hmm," she'd murmur occasionally.

The cameraman moved to the other side of the couch and shot reverse close-ups of the old woman over Ginger's shoulder. Then he told Ginger to simply talk to the old lady while he drifted around the room getting various long shots that they could use as cutting pieces where they would edit. He also took a close-up of a framed photograph on the windowsill—two skinny, mustachioed men in their late thirties who looked older, with insincere gap-toothed smiles and hard, feral eyes. The kind of men you'd cross the street to avoid, or who would cause you to leave a bar or tavern by the very act of their entering it. Roy and Troy Keighley—missing. That'd be a good shot to use while the old lady talked about what good boys they were.

"We really appreciate your taking the time to see us, Mrs. Keighley," Ginger was saying. "Someone will be contacting you, and we might want to come back and talk to you some more. Would that be all right?"

"I jus' want justice," the old woman said.

Finally, after another five minutes, it was over. The two men unclipped the microphones, disconnected their various electrical devices and packed everything up into neat pewter-colored cases. "Be sure to watch yourself on the six o'clock news," Ginger said by way of good-bye.

And then they were gone. The old woman remained sitting on the couch for a few minutes, motionless. Then she fanned herself with her hand.

Outside, the TV crew was shooting "bumpers," an introduction and then a follow-up to the interview they'd just conducted. Ginger stood across the street from the apartment building so the cameraman could get it in the shot, looking very serious and professional, her hand-held microphone just below chin level so it wouldn't block her face.

She talked for about thirty seconds and then said with finality, "Virginia Carville, Channel 12 News." The camera and microphone were turned off and the two men loaded the equipment into the back of the light blue Channel 12 van. Ginger pulled off her suit jacket. Her white blouse was soaked, the white slip beneath it showing through. She'd have to hang the blouse up to dry before going on the air in the studio at six o'clock.

"That's dynamite," she said. "Pure gold."

"They'll never let you use it, babe," the audio guy said. "Joe Rubio's lawyer'd be all over you like ants on a dropped Tootsie Pop."

"Why?"

"You can't just accuse some guy of murder on television."

"You think I didn't check with legal before I dragged all the way out here? *We* didn't accuse anybody of anything—*she* did. We're just reporting the news." She looked at her watch. "Come on, let's hustle—we're due at the county prosecutor's office in fifteen minutes."

Finally the old woman switched on the TV, but she wasn't really watching it. A soap opera in which all the characters were forty years younger than she; Geraldo Rivera, followed by Phil Donahue, both of whom were enraged about something in which she had no interest or even understanding. She was thinking about her boys.

She did miss them something terrible, even though they'd been a caution to her from the day they were born. Roy, the oldest, had always been mean as a snake, even as a little boy, always quick with the fists. When Troy had come along three years later, he'd been Roy's natural prey, forcing him to grow up fast, even tougher and meaner than his brother just so he could survive. She'd been called into the principal's office to discuss their misbehavior so many times that it had been a relief to her when they'd dropped out of school.

But they'd always been good to her, naturally protective of her, and they'd never blamed her for the bad things she'd done, she'd *had* to do, with men. After the father had walked out on her, when Troy was four years old, it had been the only way she knew to keep food on the table, and they'd understood that and never thought badly of her.

Later when they grew up, they always seemed to have money, even though neither one ever held a job for more than a few months, but they'd never been very generous and sharing with her, except for an occasional crumb—ten dollars here, five dollars there. She'd lied to the TV woman about that—but she wasn't going to say bad things about her boys on television, not now that they were gone.

She hated Joseph Rubio. He had no right to hurt her boys, just like he had no right to the money. There were always people like Rubio who lived off the work and sweat of others, and when you were poor and powerless, you just had to sit by and take it. Sometimes.

She went to the tiny kitchen and pried open a can of beans. Because of her teeth there weren't too many things she could eat anymore, and beans were soft in the mouth and filling. She heated them up on the hotplate in a pan of water without taking them out of the can, and while they were cooking she put butter substitute on two slices of day-old bread—it had been day-old when she bought it, but now it was several days more ancient—and put everything on a plate from a set of Mel Mac she'd bought twenty-five years ago. Taking a fork from the mismatched collection in her kitchen drawer she went back out and sat on the sofa again, her dinner plate resting on her lap, and waited for the six o'clock news.

There was that blond woman, that Vivian, talking about

the president, but Mrs. Keighley had little comprehension of what the story had to say. She mashed the beans to mush with the tines of the fork and started taking slow bites, chewing as best she could. She sopped up some of the liquid from the beans with the bread because it made it easier to eat as well.

That good-looking man who was on the news every day was in the mayor's office talking about something else now, but again she had no interest in it.

"Locally, a big story of a West Side woman whose two sons have been missing for three months and has made a startling accusation. Here with that exclusive report is Virginia Carville," that Vivian was saying.

There was the lady that had been in her apartment that afternoon, standing outside the building and saying, "Mrs. Rose Keighley called Channel 12 News this morning with an accusation that her two sons, Roy and Troy Keighley, missing since the beginning of May, are actually murder victims. Mrs. Keighley accuses Joseph Rubio, who just yesterday was convicted of dealing illegal drugs after one of the biggest drug busts in Cleveland history last June. We talked to her here in her home on West 103rd Street."

And then there she herself was on the screen, sitting on this very sofa with that lady. The lady looked prettier on television than she did in person, Mrs. Keighley thought. As for the way *she* looked, it made her sad. She knew she'd been pretty once, when all those men were coming around. Now she looked old; well, she *was* old, but there were some people who were old and didn't look it. People who had enough money to fix themselves up and stay healthy.

She felt vaguely disoriented seeing and hearing herself like this. She thought she'd said some things to the lady that they didn't put on the television, but she wasn't sure; her memory wasn't what it used to be.

"We talked to County Prosecutor Gerald Duitsman about the disappearance of the Keighley brothers in his office at the Justice Center this afternoon," the lady was saying, and then all of a sudden she wasn't in Mrs. Keighley's living room anymore, but in an austere-looking office, talking to a slim, balding man in a gray suit who was sitting behind a big, important-looking desk.

"This office will be looking into the allegations," he said, "but frankly, without any hard evidence, without any bodies, there won't be much we can do, legally. Roy and Troy Keighley were known drug dealers and on Rubio's payroll, but that in and of itself isn't enough to prepare an indictment against Rubio."

And then there she was again, twisting her skinny hands on her lap, and the lady was saying off-screen, "So Rose Keighley waits—living on her meager Social Security pension and hoping—without much hope—that her two sons are still alive."

A big close-up, her face filling the screen, showing every wrinkle, every tear, even the two long white hairs sprouting from her chin, and Mrs. Keighley looked away from the television in dismay as she heard herself saying, "Roy an' Troy, they was good boys."

That Vivian came on again, so perfect and pretty, as though she never broke wind or broke a sweat, and said, "Thank you for that exclusive report, Virginia. When we come back, Colin Brannigan has news of a major trade by the Indians."

The TV lady had it wrong. She wasn't hoping they'd come back, not any more. She knew they wouldn't. They'd told her that they hadn't stolen the money, that they'd lost it, but that Rubio would get them for it anyway. And when they hadn't come home that night, May Three, she knew that their worst fears had been realized. She'd been afraid to come forward before, but now that Rubio was in prison she wanted her revenge for what had happened to Roy and Troy. That's the only reason she'd go on the TV looking terrible the way she did. For revenge.

The screen cut to a commercial—some man yelling about carpets. The old woman put her plate on the floor beside her and rose with difficulty. She went into the tiny bedroom and into the closet. On her knees she brushed aside the dust bunnies and shoes and carpet slippers with her hands like a dog digging up a bone, finally uncovering the loose baseboard in the corner of the closet. She pulled it aside and extracted the three bundles she'd hidden there.

She didn't need to count it; she knew exactly how much was there. Thirty-two thousand, eight hundred and seventy dollars, mostly in hundreds and fifties. She'd counted it a million times before. But she liked to look at it, and since her eyes weren't so good anymore she liked the tactile sense of it, to riffle the edges of the bills. It made her feel good to know that Joseph Rubio would never get his hands on it, not after her boys had done all the work, all the collecting, taken all the chances out there on the street with a bunch of crazy people who'd just as soon shoot you as look at you. Now it could do some good for a decent person, augmenting the Social Security and maybe buying her a warm new coat for the winter to come, maybe a little stew meat once in a while. It gave her an almost maternal comfort to hold it, now that Roy and Troy were gone.

Poor Roy and Troy, she thought, sniffling back a new freshet of tears. That Rubio had no call to hurt them any. *They* hadn't taken his old money. They wouldn't do anything like that.

They were such good boys.

For a very short time in 1992–1993, there existed a little weekly newspaper in Cleveland called City Reports, *for which I was allowed to give my curmudgeonly side full reign and write a weekly column on whatever happened to tick me off. The paper was too grown-up for the counter-culture, not immediate enough for the hard news buffs, and not entertaining enough for the guy next door, and it folded quietly.*

On its last Christmas, City Reports *published two short-short stories of the season, mine and another local writer's. I don't remember now what I originally entitled mine, but, I suppose because they called hers "Angel of Mercy," they re-titled mine "Angel of Death," a title I hate an awful lot.*

Angel of Death

Sonny Della Fiore didn't know how to do Christmas. He'd never really done it before, at least not within memory. Not since before his mother died when he was nine, leaving him in the hands of a father who seemed never to be sober.

After that he was on the Brooklyn streets, stealing what he could and running errands for the mob until old Sean Green himself—Red Green, everyone called him because of the color of his hair—took a liking to him and brought him up through the organization and sent him to school to learn bookkeeping.

So well did Sonny absorb his lessons that around Brooklyn they used to call him "The Laundryman" for his skill at cleaning off dirty money. They were fond of saying that he not only washed it, but ironed it as well.

But a lot of ambitious people run around during an election year making noises about organized crime, and a hotshot young prosecutor from the Brooklyn RICO squad who had down-the-road dreams of the governor's mansion followed the Laundryman's well-concealed paper trail and came down on Sonny like a wrathful Jehovah.

The prosecutor wasn't after bookkeepers. He had bigger fish to fry, so when he offered Sonny a deal that would keep him out of a federal penitentiary for eight years or so, Sonny folded up and gave him Red Green.

He had spent the last Christmas in protective custody.

A New England Christmas it was, in a small Vermont town. The pretty, picture-book snow and children caroling and sledding outside were painful to him because he couldn't even poke his head out of the house—but then Christmas never meant much to Sonny anyway. There'd always been an envelope from Red, and maybe a sweater or tie from whomever he was running with that year, but no real holiday feel to it.

And then came the Federal Witness Protection Program. That was part of the deal, because even in the joint, Red Green had a long arm. And a longer memory.

First the plastic surgery—they shortened his nose and took out the hump, but Sonny, always vain, wouldn't let them do much else. They put him through weeks of electrolysis to alter his hairline and his eyebrows, and that was more painful than the nose job, Sonny thought. They fitted him with contact lenses to make his brown eyes green, they gave him what seemed to be a lifetime supply of Lady Clairol to change the color of his hair, and they arranged a new job and Social Security number and a brand new identity.

Stanley Flowers. Bookkeeper to a small electronics firm in Solon, Ohio, just outside Cleveland.

Stanley, for God's sake.

He'd beefed about what he considered a dorky name, but the feds had pointed out that no self-respecting hoodlum would choose a name like Stanley Flowers if he could help it, and because of that it was an ideal cover.

But to his surprise Sonny—Stanley—had taken to life in the straight world. Solon was a pretty place, the people were warm and welcoming to a newcomer, and it wasn't that far a drive into Cleveland to catch an occasional ballgame or a show. They'd found him a nice little house to rent with honest-to-God rose bushes in the front yard, given him a low-mileage two-year-old Chevy Corsica, and he was able to save some money.

After about six months he even stopped worrying that Red Green's people would find him. No more looking over his shoulder, no more jumping at the sound of the telephone, no more peeking out the door before venturing onto the street, and no more cold sweats when he turned the key in his car's ignition and waited for the bomb blast. He knew about Red Green's paybacks.

It was lonely for a while. Most of his co-workers were nice enough, but married, and hung out with married friends, so he spent weekends in the house watching sports, or working in the garden. He'd planted rows of hosta on either side of the walk leading to his front door, and in the spring he'd peeled off and replaced the wallpaper in his living room.

Then just after Thanksgiving Jane Lang came to work for his company. She'd smiled shyly at him when they were introduced, but he hadn't noticed; at first glance she wasn't very noticeable, with her baggy cardigan sweaters and mouse-colored hair. But after she'd been there about a week he happened to catch her with her big glasses off, and he couldn't help remarking on how large and pretty her eyes were, a kind of deep blue with dark circles around the irises.

And then he noticed that beneath the cardigans and loose skirts she had a slim, lithe body he found most interesting, and that her hair was soft and shining and moved prettily when she turned her head.

After another week he asked her out.

It was a quiet Friday night in a family-type restaurant just off the freeway. She ordered iced tea, and he followed her lead even though he wanted a bourbon. He encouraged her to talk about herself because he couldn't very well discuss his own past. But he found himself anxious to hear about her, about her family in Indiana, and about her dreams.

When he took her back to her apartment he didn't make a move. He didn't even kiss her goodnight—at least not a real kiss, but kind of a quick hug and a peck on the cheek. All the way home he thought about the way her hair smelled.

They went out twice a week after that, dinner or a movie or once a take-out pizza with Monday Night Football. Things had advanced from cheek kisses to deep, soulful ones, and once while kissing goodnight at her door, he ventured a quick feel through her heavy winter coat, but it went no further, and surprisingly enough that was okay with Sonny.

He'd never been out with a woman more than three times and not gone to bed with her, but there was just something about Jane—she seemed so nice, so innocent. Not someone you just nailed casually and then forgot about. He wanted to go slowly; he wanted it to be right. Jane was becoming very dear to him.

So it was only natural that he wanted to spend Christmas Eve with her.

Except for a bottle of booze to the doorman at his

Brooklyn apartment, he'd never given anyone a Christmas gift before. He didn't know how to proceed.

Jewelry seemed a little excessive, especially from a guy who was supposed to be only a bookkeeper. He considered clothing, but he was afraid she'd think it was too intimate. Yet a book or an audiotape was so damned impersonal, and kitchen appliances were what people bought their mothers.

He settled on a silk scarf—blue to match her eyes.

She got into the car carrying a lavishly wrapped present, red and green metallic paper and a big silk bow. He felt ashamed at his own inept gift-wrapping, the Scotch tape applied unevenly and a cheap stick-on bow on top.

"Let's drive out to the lake and open them," she suggested with all the glee of a ten-year-old, and so smitten was he that he agreed, even though that wasn't what he had planned.

"Me first," she said when they were parked in a deserted campground by the lake. He'd left the ignition on so they could stay warm and enjoy the carols on the car radio.

She gushed over the scarf and immediately tied it around her neck, and he was pleased to see he'd been right about her eyes. "Merry Christmas," he said, and then almost fearfully added a tentative "honey." The word felt good—it felt right.

Sonny Della Fiore—Stanley Flowers—was falling in love.

His package felt heavy, substantial. When he began opening it she scolded, "Don't wreck it now—the bow's so pretty. Here, let me . . ."

She carefully slid off the bow and took off the paper with a minimum of damage, revealing a plain white box about a foot square. She looked at him teasingly, her eyes dancing, as she slowly lifted the lid, holding the box so he couldn't see inside it.

The anticipation of his first real Christmas gift was driving him crazy. "Well?" he finally said with a laugh.

Jane took out a small nickel-plated .22 handgun, and it gleamed in the light of the dashboard instrumentation.

For a moment he didn't understand.

But when she said "Merry Christmas, squealer—from Red," just before she pulled the trigger, just before the bullet slammed into his brain, he did.

I chose this as the "title story" for this collection because it's just about my favorite of all my titles. Written for Martin H. Greenberg and Ed Gorman's second Cat Crimes *anthology, it was actually inspired by a car trip I took across country, during which I flirted shamelessly with an attractive woman in the next car for some ninety miles across the state of Kansas. We finally wound up at the same gas station, had an iced tea together, and went our separate ways. But writers, I've found, are like a Native American carving up a buffalo—nothing goes to waste.*

The Scent of Spiced Oranges

He'd been playing bumper tag with the blonde in the old tan Subaru with California plates for over an hour on Interstate 70, starting about noon east of Denver and continuing on across the state line and into the middle of Kansas. That particular stretch of highway is probably the dullest in the world, a drive-through sensory-deprivation experience, flat and brown and lonely, and before the blonde he'd found himself wondering how many miles it was going to be until the next tree.

He'd noticed her when she came down the on-ramp to the interstate, a sexy-looking woman in her late twenties, wearing a big straw sun hat with a curly blond ponytail threaded through the open back of it, and a maroon halter top. As he sped by her he noticed that every inch of the Subaru was packed with clothes, books and blankets—probably every-

55

thing she owned. It looked like one of those cars from *The Grapes of Wrath.*

What really got his attention was the cat. It was an orange tabby with eyes the same color, and it prowled atop the blonde's belongings like a sentry, easily keeping its balance in the speeding car. The summer highways of the United States normally carry the cars and RVs of senior citizens who have an unlimited amount of time and a limited amount of money for their vacations; a pretty blonde with an orange cat was enough of a rarity to attract his notice. And he was the kind of man who always noticed good-looking women, wherever they were.

A few minutes after she'd integrated into the stream of traffic, she roared past him on the left and, aware of his gaze, glanced over at him, a small smile on her lips. He noticed that the car windows were open just a hairline crack at the top. She must not have an air conditioner, he thought, but she has to keep the windows shut because of the cat.

When she'd gotten about twenty yards ahead of him she drifted back into the right lane, and they drove along like that for about five minutes while he wondered idly what a California woman was doing in the middle of Kansas with all her worldly goods and a muscular-looking orange tabby.

There were two slow-moving trucks and a camper ahead of her, and she pulled out into the left lane, accelerating to at least ten miles over the speed limit as she passed them. He followed her, noticing as he swept by the camper that it was being driven by an elderly woman with a face like a persimmon, wearing a baseball cap. As the blonde moved back into the right lane ahead of the camper, he went by her too, and as he looked over at her she gave him a radiantly mischievous smile, acknowledging that they were hop scotching each other every few minutes and that she was enjoying the game. The cat just glared.

As he returned to the right lane he saw in his mirror that she was still smiling. She was pretty cute, he thought, and in the manner of some married men away from home, he began fantasizing about her, about how he could get to meet her, how he could make his move.

He tapped the brake until he was doing about sixty-two miles an hour and cruised there awhile, waiting for her to pull up beside him. When she did he tried to catch her eye, drinking in dumb show, hoping she'd get off at the next exit and have a Coke with him, but this time she didn't make eye contact or even slow down, and at that speed he couldn't keep looking over at her without swerving onto the gravelly shoulder of the road.

He watched helplessly as she pulled far ahead of him. When they reached the next exit, a small town called Victoria, he noticed she didn't pull off. She hadn't seen his pantomime.

The station he'd found on the radio was fading in and out on him now, the curse of the traveling man while driving in remote rural areas. He had a tape player in the car but he never used it. He didn't care that much about music, anyway—all that interested him were the weather and traffic advisories and the sports news. He punched angrily at the "Seek" button until he found another clear station— country music, which he loathed, but they'd probably do a newscast on the half-hour. He started thinking about the sales he'd made in Denver yesterday, and the call he would make tomorrow afternoon in Indianapolis. That he'd sell them was a given; he always sold this particular company. The only thing in question was the amount. In his head he was calculating the various commissions he had earned and might earn, depending on the mood of the buyer, and he fig- ured he'd have enough to spring for a high-priced lunch before getting the order and heading home to Columbus and his wife.

He passed the flattened carcass of what used to be a dog. He refused to look at it, and shuddered. He never got used to seeing dead things, even though road kill was as much a feature of the scenery as wheat fields. Kansas, it seemed to him, was the dead dog capital of the world.

The sun was high and relentless, giving the landscape the look of a color snapshot that had been overexposed, and the pavement ahead of him shimmered, mesmerizing him. He'd been fortunate on this trip not to have run into too much road construction, those orange barrels blocking one of the two lanes that slowed him down and left him drumming his fingers on the steering wheel in frustration. It was bad enough driving through the endless monotony of the Great Plains at top speed, but to crawl along eating the dust of the car in front of him was intolerable.

He checked his watch to find he'd been on the road for three hours without a break, and then glanced down at the fuel gauge, which was only one-quarter full. He decided to make an all-purpose pit stop at the next town—gasoline, the rest room, and a cold drink.

He rolled into a Shell station in Russell, Kansas, at about three o'clock, and when he got out of the car the heat struck him like a fist. He stuck the gas nozzle into the tank and leaned against the fender as the numbers clicked off on the pump. When it stopped automatically he returned the hose to its niche, screwed the cap back on the tank, and went inside to pay and use the john. On the way out he pulled a can of Pepsi out of the cooler.

When he got back to his car the blonde in the Subaru was just pulling up to an adjacent pump. She rolled her window down, glancing over her shoulder to make sure the cat didn't jump out. But it was resting sphinx-like atop a wicker basket and seemed disinterested in the whole thing.

"Well, hello," he said.

Her laugh tinkled like wind chimes. "Oh, hi," she said. "I thought we'd lost each other." She extended a languid arm out of the window, and when he moved to shake it he could see she was wearing loose-legged white shorts. "I'm Rose."

The restaurant across from the Shell station was almost empty in the midday lull between late lunch and early dinner, and the waitress was trying hard to talk them into trying the buffet dinner for $5.95. They resisted, ordering only iced tea for him and herbal tea for her. She squeezed lemon into hers while he loaded his glass with sugar.

"Actually I'd passed this exit," she was saying, "and then I looked down and realized I needed some gas and Widget needed some water."

"Widget?"

"My kitty," she explained. "I got off a few miles down the road but there were no stations, so I just took the service road and doubled back here." Her eyes twinkled as she looked at him from beneath the visor of her sun hat. "Now I'm glad I did."

"Where you headed, Rose?" he said.

"I'm going to Lee's Summit. It's just the other side of Kansas City."

"What's in Lee's Summit?"

"Peace, I hope. I'm a healer."

"You're a doctor?"

"No, no. A healer. Laying on of hands, meditation, that kind of thing."

He sipped his iced tea and nodded thoughtfully, trying to look interested, thinking it was just his luck to pick up a nut case. Well, if his luck was running, perhaps he could talk her into laying some hands on him. And vice versa.

"I've been living in L.A. for the past three years and I got to hating it a lot," she said. "But you know how it is—you want to get out but you've got no place to go. Finally I just ran out of money. So I wrote this friend of mine in Lee's Summit and she invited me to come and stay as long as I liked." She shrugged, her breasts lifting in their halter, and his eyes followed their rise and fall, the delicate tracery of blue veins beneath tanned skin. Her perfume rose from them, and he leaned forward to get a better whiff. He couldn't quite place it, but it seemed appropriate somehow, a California kind of smell.

"I've got a great idea," he said, consulting his watch. "Let's drive on for another couple of hours until we get to Kansas City, and have dinner together. On me."

"Don't you have to be somewhere?"

"As long as I hit Indianapolis before five o'clock tomorrow I'll be fine," he said.

She chewed on her lip. "I don't know. I really need to be focused on what I'm going to do in Lee's Summit—I shouldn't let anything distract me."

"You've got to eat anyway, don't you? Look, it'll be a nice change for me. I'm always on the road—I spend my whole life eating alone in restaurants." He gave her his best little-boy-lost look. "I'd really like the company." He didn't add that since she'd run out of money she ought to jump at the chance of a free meal, but he was thinking it.

She brushed the hair out of her face. She'd taken off the hat and at close range he could see the network of tiny lines around her eyes and at the corners of her mouth; she was older than he'd thought, maybe late thirties. But she was still pretty cute, and a married guy couldn't be too choosy.

She gave him that tinkly laugh again. "Well—I guess it'd be all right."

He gulped down the rest of his tea and slurped the sugar at the bottom of the glass, glowing with satisfaction and anticipation. He'd always been good at closing a sale.

They crossed the state line four hours later. As a traveling man it always amused him that each state you enter by car has an enormous sign that bids you welcome to their friendly scenic wonders, and a hundred yards farther another sign advising what they'll do to you if you break the traffic laws. He hoped Rose had noticed the second sign; he'd been following her long enough to know that she drove pretty fast when she thought no one was watching, and he certainly didn't want her stopped for a speeding ticket. He had other plans.

The steak house on the Missouri side of Kansas City was one he'd heard of but never visited before. He wanted to be sure he didn't run into anyone he knew who might also know his wife. It was unlikely in Kansas City, but there was no such thing as being too careful.

He had two martinis before dinner and they both ordered T-bone rib steaks with baked potato. He selected a medium-priced St. Emillion to go with the meal; he'd never heard of the wine before but he figured it would impress her. She took desultory sips of hers and he wound up finishing the bottle. It made him bold. All during dinner he kept dropping not-so-subtle double entendres, and she laughed dutifully at each of them. He figured he was a pretty funny guy.

When they'd finished dinner he suggested coffee and a brandy.

"I don't drink either one," she said. "But you go ahead, have what you want."

"I always do," he leered, taking her hand and giving it a little squeeze, then running up her bare arm with his fingers.

She giggled, batting her lashes. He wound up having two brandies and barely touching the coffee, and Rose asked the waitress for a "kitty bag" and inserted the steak bone into it with long, slim fingers.

Before paying the bill he went to the men's room, feeling more than a little woozy. In the stall he checked the cash in his pocket. Two hundred sixty-seven dollars. That was good. He had a company credit card in his wallet, and two of his own, but he didn't want to leave any sort of paper trail that could be questioned by his boss or his wife.

When he got back to the table, Rose said, "I didn't know it was so late. Oh, this is terrible."

"Why?"

"It's almost eleven. I can't walk in on my friend at nearly midnight, not when she's being kind enough to put me up."

He sat back, his full belly pushing against the front of his white shirt, visions of sugarplums dancing drunkenly in his head. "No problem," he said, throwing three twenties and a few singles on the table next to the bill. "I have to get a motel room anyway."

He had the motel picked out ahead of time. It was in Independence, Missouri, and he had passed it a hundred times on the way through, although he'd never stayed there. Their sign proclaimed rooms from fifteen dollars up, and since the company paid his expenses he always stayed somewhere a little more posh. But tonight was going to be out-of-pocket, and he was nothing if not frugal. After all, he'd already blown more than sixty dollars on dinner.

It was a big motel, more than a hundred units, and he pulled up to a parking spot on the side of the building, noting with satisfaction that she was right behind him.

He climbed out of his car, a wave of dizziness making him

stumble a little. He really did have a lot to drink with dinner. "I'll go register," he said.

She nodded her acquiescence and started to gather whatever she'd need for the night from the jumble of belongings on the seat beside her. Despite the heat he rubbed his hands together in anticipation.

"A room for two," he told the clerk, a young girl who looked to be just out of school. "King-size bed if you got one." When she pushed the registration card toward him, he signed it "Richard Thompson, Akron, Ohio," which was neither his name nor his hometown. He put down a false license number, too. And he paid in cash.

The room was down toward the far end of the building, and he thought about driving down there, but his head was buzzing and he didn't feel like getting into the car again. He grabbed his overnight case and locked the car. Rose stood waiting for him, a large purse her only luggage, the cat cradled in her arms against her breasts.

"You're not bringing him in with us?" he said.

Her eyes widened. "You don't expect the poor kitty to stay in that stuffy car all night, do you?"

He didn't like cats. He'd never trusted them, and he didn't like the way they smelled. But the heat in his loins was his priority right then, so he shrugged and took her arm to lead her down the walkway.

The room was virtually indistinguishable from ten thousand other such rooms lining the interstate highways of America—gray carpeting, off-white walls, imitation blond veneer dresser, too-thin towels and miniature rectangles of Dial soap. The loudly humming air conditioner was blasting icy air, and his damp shirt turned instantly cold and clammy. He shut the door and put his arms around her, nuzzling in her neck. Her perfume made him giddy, and he thought he identified the scent now—the smell of spiced oranges. She tried to squirm away but he forced his tongue into her mouth, one hand behind her head and the other cupping her buttocks. He ground his body against her.

"I've been wanting to do this since the first time I saw you on the highway," he said. He could hear the slurring of his own words.

"Take it easy, lover," she said finally, out of breath. She pushed him away. "So have I, but I've been on the road all day. A girl needs to freshen up a little, you know?"

She caressed his face with one hand and gave him a fleeting kiss as she disappeared into the bathroom.

He stood in the middle of the room, swaying a bit, tasting the brandy at the back of his throat. He went over and stood directly in front of the air conditioner, letting it blow on his face until he got his bearings again. Widget, the cat, rubbed itself against his leg, and he moved away, startled. The cat prowled the room, sniffing, its tail an orange question mark above its back.

He heard the water running in the bathroom, and a loopy smile twisted his mouth. He turned down the bed; the sheets were stiff with sizing, a drab institutional white, and had seen better days. He stripped off all his clothes, leaving them in a pile on the floor, and after a quick look in the mirror on the dresser and sucking in his gut to its flatness of twenty years ago, turned off the light and slipped under the covers, appropriating both pillows to put beneath his head.

He lay there for a while, impatient for her to finish. He closed his eyes, fantasizing. In his imaginings he wasn't drunk anymore, and he imagined how she'd come out of the bathroom, how she'd look, what she'd do, what he would do to her. It was a delicious dream, at first almost violent in its passion and then slow and sensuous and lazy. So lazy . . .

A sudden weight on his feet brought him out of it; the cat had jumped up on the bed and was kneading the blanket with its sharp little claws. He could hear the gentle, soft rhythm of its purring. His eyelids were heavy from the alcohol, and with great effort he forced them open.

She was at the foot of the bed, fully dressed except for the straw hat, with her purse over one arm. She was holding his trousers, going through the pockets, and as though he was viewing a movie that had nothing to do with him, he watched as she extracted what was left of his money.

It wasn't until she scooped the cat off the bed with her free hand and started for the door that he really woke up and achieved full cognizance that he had been suckered. Set up like some small-town chump away from home for the first time. Naked, he vaulted out of bed and across the floor in one motion, his hands reaching for her, pawing at her, but there was nothing erotic about it anymore. He wanted what she'd taken from him. "Hey!" he said.

She dropped the cat and tried to struggle out of his grasp. She was quicksilver to hold on to, all elbows and knees, as he tried to wrench the money from her fist. "Let go!" he rasped through teeth clenched so tight that it gave him a headache.

One of her knees pistoned up hard between his legs, making him grunt, and in pain and anger he hurled her away from him. She staggered a few steps, her feet tangling in his trousers on the floor, and she fell, the back of her head striking the sharp corner of the dresser on her way down.

He pounced on her, prying her fingers apart and snatching the money away from her. Then he straightened up, his chest heaving with the unaccustomed exertion. He turned back to her. "Get up," he panted. "And get out."

She didn't move. The cat prowled around her, nudging her with its nose.

"Come on, Rose."

She still didn't stir, and all at once the goose flesh on his bare chest wasn't from the chill of the air conditioner anymore.

He knelt down beside her, brushing the cat roughly away from her with the back of his hand. A faint glow from the lights in the parking lot was seeping through the drape on the window, but it was enough for him to see the dark pool spreading beneath her head. He was careful not to touch it. He didn't have to; he knew what it was. Her eyes stared sightlessly at the pebbled ceiling, her mouth an **O** of horror. He put his palm on her chest just under her left breast and didn't feel a heartbeat. He hadn't expected to. The cat, not minding the rebuff, licked at the puddle beneath the blonde's head.

He leaped upright again, his heart like a hammer in his chest, and ran for the bathroom, his insides contracting violently. Before he was finished his stomach was completely empty and he was bathed in sweat again.

He went back into the room. He couldn't catch his breath, and for a few moments he moved frantically around, gasping like a beached fish. Uncomfortable with his nakedness, he pulled on his trousers, and leaned against the wall next to the bed, the love handles of middle age spilling over his waistband. He made a conscious effort to relax, willing himself to, and after a time he was able to breathe again.

He went to the telephone on the nightstand, next to the imitation leather-covered Bible thoughtfully provided by the Gideons. He figured the police emergency number was 911, as it was in most cities. But his hand hovered over the receiver and finally fell to his side.

He was in trouble.

Even if no criminal charges were filed against him, this would certainly cost him his marriage. His wife would understand him trying to save his money, but after twelve years of marriage to a man who had been known to stray before she wouldn't be quite so accepting about what he was doing in a motel room with Rose in the first place.

And there went his house, his car, and half his income.

He was also sure his job would evaporate like raindrops in a summer heat; his boss was a straitlaced type, a pillar of the Methodist Church, and would take a pretty dim view of what happened. If he called the police now, he would be ruined twenty ways from Sunday.

He sank down on the bed and rubbed his eyes with his fingers, trying to ease the savage pounding behind them so he could think. He kept his eyes averted from the woman's body on the floor, just as he had with the dead dog on the highway, as though if he didn't look at it, didn't acknowledge it was there, it wouldn't be, and he would be alone in the room, no Rose and no Widget, watching a movie on cable and nodding off before the last reel. Just an ordinary stopover between Denver and Indianapolis.

Then he started to think about it. No one had seen him with the woman except the waitress in Kansas City. He had paid cash for both dinner and the room and falsified the registration card in the motel office. He was practically untraceable.

Spirits soaring, he rushed into the bathroom where the lingering smell of her spiced orange perfume was a silent rebuke. He washed away the vestiges of his sickness with the motel washcloth, then rinsed it out in hot water and laid it over the shower rod to dry. With a towel he wiped down almost every surface in the room, even though he'd undressed and gotten into bed immediately and couldn't remember touching anything. The heady jolt of fear kept him moving quickly, despite the fact that he was exhausted and still half-drunk.

He had pulled his trousers on quickly, and now he took them off and put on his underwear, his shirt, and the rest of his clothes. They were damp and sweaty, but he didn't care. He put the roll of bills in his pocket, picked up his wallet from the floor where she'd dropped it during her search, grabbed his overnight case and went out, being careful to wipe off the door handles and jamb. He thought about looking back at the woman's body one last time, but fought the impulse off.

When he got into his car he didn't look over at her Subaru, either. He was going to put the whole episode out of his mind, he thought.

It was quiet in the parking lot and almost all of the rooms were dark behind their drapes. He started the engine, turned on the air conditioner, and drove out of the lot with his lights off. He almost didn't remember to turn them on when he went down the ramp onto Interstate 70 half a block away. Heading west—back the way he'd come.

He was going to get a hotel room back in Kansas some-place, maybe in Lawrence or Topeka, just in case. Then he could say he hadn't even reached Independence at the approximate time the woman was killed. It was a ruse that could easily be broken by a relentless police investigator, but he didn't think it would even come close to that. There was no way anyone could connect a traveling salesman from Columbus, Ohio, with a whacked-out cat-loving faith healer from Los Angeles. It would mean an extra-long drive in the morning, but he'd get an early start.

The fact that he'd snuffed out a human life was not lost on him; it lay heavy in his stomach like a cold smooth stone. But like an alcoholic in denial he manufactured a whole set of excuses for himself. If she hadn't smiled so radiantly at him on the highway he never would have bothered with her. She had probably seen him leave the interstate back at the Shell station and had doubled back to find him, larceny in her heart from the very beginning. Healer my foot, he thought—hustler is more like it.

She'd been good at it, he had to give her that. She'd beaten him out of an expensive meal, tried to steal his money while he slept, and perhaps worst of all, had not delivered the reward he'd been expecting. She probably did this all the time, made her living at it. She deserved what she got.

He had driven about fifteen miles before the anxiety attack hit, and he had to pull off onto the right shoulder until he stopped hyperventilating and his hands quit shaking. He would have been happy to stay there all night, safe in his little steel cocoon while traffic roared by him, but he didn't want a state highway cop stopping by to see what the trouble was. With enormous effort he got control of himself and resumed his westward trek.

He switched on the radio, twisting the dial until he could get clear reception, but he was unaware of the music, "Judy's Turn to Cry" on a rock oldies station. His eyes kept flickering up to the mirror, but there was no one following him, very little traffic of any kind after midnight. Every once in a while a big semi would rumble past him, spouting diesel fumes, its side lights and tail lights and running lights like a kid's carnival ride in the blackness.

As he negotiated the interstate where it threaded its way directly through downtown Kansas City and across the Missouri River for the second time that day, he kept a worried eye on the speedometer. Most highway cops gave you a five mile grace, but he kept the needle at fifty-five. He didn't want to chance getting stopped, still under the influence of alcohol.

And he was exhausted, too, wrung out; he nodded at the wheel, his head falling forward on his chest and then snapping up again. He rubbed his eyes and slapped his own face gently. He was too experienced a long distance driver to go on like that much longer; he had seen too many twisted, burned wrecks at the side of the road. He had to get some sleep.

A green sign told him that Lawrence, Kansas, was twelve miles ahead. He'd stopped there for lunch once or twice, a nice quiet college town a few miles south of the highway, with several motels cheek-by-jowl with the truck stops and gasoline stations and ubiquitous fast-food restaurants. He turned up the music and the cold air and took a deep breath. He could make it.

Twenty minutes later he was driving the main drag of Lawrence, batting his eyes to stay awake and gritting his teeth at the proliferation of NO VACANCY signs at all the motels. What was the big deal about Lawrence, Kansas, on this particular evening? he wondered. It was midweek, midsummer, no homecoming weekend or football game. He tried not to take it personally, but then he tended to take everything personally, as if society in general had teamed up with the gods to make his life tough.

At the end of the strip he found a Best Western whose red sign told him there was a room available, and he docked his car in front of the office. Not a moment too soon, either, he thought. His eyelids were heavy and his brain was dangerously overloaded.

The kid behind the desk was obviously clerking as a summer job, and he handed him a registration card and a pen, watching while he used his real name and address.

"Credit card, sir?"

"Sure," he said, rotating his head around until his neck popped. He could never remember being so wiped out. All he could think of was the crisp white sheets and the air-conditioned room he had just signed for. He pulled out his wallet and flipped it open, and his stomach wrenched inside him as if someone had pulled taut a rawhide cord around his large intestine.

The credit cards were gone.

That's why she'd dropped the wallet on the floor—she'd removed the credit cards before she went into his pants pockets for the money. They were probably in her own pocket or purse right now where she lay on the institutional gray carpet of the Independence motel.

He heard a sound coming out of his throat that he tried to cover with a cough. "No, ah—never mind, I changed my—"

He snatched the registration card from the startled clerk, crumpled it up and jammed it into his hip pocket, and rushed out the door to his car.

He had to get back to Independence before anyone found her, had to get those credit cards and whatever else she might have removed from his wallet that had his name on it.

This time he didn't worry about holding down his speed on the highway, he wasn't worried about anything except getting back to that motel room. His head bobbed with exhaustion, but his foot remained steady on the accelerator pedal. He was angry with himself—he had nearly blown it.

As he was driving through Kansas City a horrifying thought struck him. How was he going to get back into the room? Sweat pouring off his face and chest heaving with the effort to breathe, he squirmed around in the car seat and plunged his hand deep into his pocket, touching the large flat plastic disc attached to the key. He sighed. One less thing to worry about.

Relief flooded over him and the tension ebbed away. He leaned his head back on the headrest, taking his first relaxed breath in more than two hours, no longer fighting the fatigue and the alcohol, no longer firing all cylinders in panic. Everything was going to be fine.

Just fine . . .

That's when he felt the little needle claws digging into his shoulder and the back of his neck, and he sucked in his breath. The damn cat had followed him out of the motel room and sneaked into his car when he wasn't looking. Startled and in pain, he twisted the wheel frantically. The last sound he heard was the soft, rattling purr next to his ear.

When the Rescue Squad cut him out of the wreckage of his car with the Jaws of Life, one of the men fished the frightened and trembling orange cat from where it huddled on the floor of the back seat. He took it home that night, and in the morning his little daughter, delighted with her new pet, decided to name it Lucky.

In 1992 I was one of the speakers at a writer's conference at Cuyahoga Community College in Cleveland. One of my fellow presenters was Kay Sloan, who taught at Miami University in Oxford, Ohio. After the conference, when we were all heading for dinner, she mentioned to me that she and Constance Pierce were editing a short story anthology dealing with Elvis Presley—not necessarily Elvis himself, but the effect he has had on American life and culture. She asked me if I'd like to contribute, but I demurred, telling her that I was never an Elvis fan; like my fictional creation Milan Jacovich, I am often called "retro," and wear the mantle proudly. My popular musical tastes stopped somewhere between Dick Haymes and Rosemary Clooney.

However, as we continued our journey across Cleveland— being the hometown kid, I was driving—the idea for this story jumped into my head almost full-blown, and I turned to her abruptly and said, "I'll do one!"

After dinner I raced home and wrote the story in one long sitting. It was during the time the U.S. Postal service was taking a poll to decide whether to release an Elvis Presley stamp showing the singer young and vital, or old and plump. (The younger version won.)

I leave it to the reader to decide exactly what the ending means.

"The Fat Stamp" first appeared in the anthology Elvis Rising *(Avon) in 1993.*

The Fat Stamp

Earl Lee didn't like Burger Kings, and that was a fact. He much preferred dining at the truck stops sprinkled along the interstates when he was doing his long-distance runs. The food was a lot better and generally so was the company. But it had been raining off and on for the last six hours, and the rhythm of the wipers on the windshield of his Pete tended to put him to sleep. That had necessitated drinking lots of coffee to stay alert as he'd rumbled down 95 from Philadelphia to just south of Richmond, where he'd picked up 85 and sliced across the Carolinas on his way to Atlanta. And every long-haul trucker understands that, like beer, you don't buy coffee, you just rent it. He'd just passed through Charlotte and was somewhere between Gastonia and Spartanburg when the pressure on his bladder had grown too strong to ignore, and the Burger King was handy.

He had just finished up his first Whopper and was starting on the second, his fingers smudged with grease and the ketchup from the large side of fries when the other trucker walked over with his tray and sat down two tables away. He was big and dark, about ten years older than Earl Lee, with eyebrows that were a single straight line across his forehead and a deeply lined face with a network of crow's feet at the corners of his eyes. He was wearing a billed, white cloth cap that said "Buy American" in red and blue letters, and the curly hair that stuck out from the back was shot through with silver.

"Hidey," Earl Lee said. He realized that except for when he'd stopped to refuel and when he'd given his order to the girl behind the counter, he hadn't spoken to another human being in almost twelve hours. And Earl Lee was a garrulous soul, not really suited to the long stretches of loneliness in the cab of his Pete.

The other trucker looked up, surprised that anyone would talk to him here in a lonely all-night fast-food joint. "Whattya say?"

Earl Lee picked up his messy tray and moved over so he was sitting at the table next to the other man. "Earl Lee Ford. Nice meetin' you."

"Hank Welk." He held out his hand but Earl Lee raised his to show him it was too greasy for a shake.

"Ain't this rain a pisscutter? Man, my eyes like to fall out of my head."

Welk unwrapped his own hamburger.

"Where you out of?"

"Winston-Salem. You?"

"Atlanta," Earl Lee told him, his mouth full of fries. "Say, you want my pickle? They give me gas."

Welk shook his head. "That's okay." They were the only two customers in the place, it being after eleven at night and past the time when most people ate hamburgers. Behind the counter two teenaged girls, one white and one black, chatted together to pass the boring off-hours. A big elderly man with a roll of fat around his middle and longish gray hair that fell into his eyes was moving among the tables with a mop, swamping up the detritus of a long and busy day.

"You follow the Braves?" Earl Lee asked.

Welk shrugged. "Much as I follow any of 'em."

Earl Lee was disappointed. Baseball was one of his best

subjects. He tried another sport. "I like the Falcons, too. They gonna have a good year, looks like."

" 'Bout damn time."

That shut Earl Lee up for a while, stung at the insult to his home team, but Welk didn't seem to notice, falling upon his sandwich as if he held a personal grudge against it.

For a time there was no sound in the restaurant except the hum of the air conditioner, the hiss of the rain outside, and the rhythmic swishing on the old swamper's mop. Earl Lee watched him for a while; he was moving his lips silently, and after much consideration Earl Lee decided he must be singing quietly to himself inside his head. He thought how sad it was a man that age had to spend his declining years mopping ketchup and Coca-Cola from the floor of a Burger King at the side of the interstate.

"You married?" he finally asked Welk.

Welk shook his huge, dark head. He looked around on the table for a moment, then reached over and took the plastic saltshaker off Earl Lee's table. He peeled the top part of his bun off the meat and covered it with a thin coating of white, then loaded his fries up with salt, too, and set to eating again.

"Me neither," Earl Lee said. "You can be married or you can push an eighteen-wheeler. Can't see no way of doing both." And then he couldn't think of anything else to say. He had to learn how to ask open-ended questions that would stimulate further conversation, he thought, instead of just yes-and-no ones. He just had to get the other man talking, or he'd walk out of here and drive another two hours, then crawl into his own lonely bed without ever talking to anyone. His need for the currency of human contact gnawed at him like a rat in his chest.

They ate for a while in silence. The antiseptic smell of whatever the fat guy was slopping on the floor was stinging

Earl Lee's nose, and the song the old man sang to himself was inaudible.

"So which Elvis stamp did you vote for?"

"Huh?"

"The Elvis Presley postage stamp. They was two of 'em, one when Elvis was young and skinny and one when he was old and fat. They had people vote for which one they wanted. I voted for the fat stamp, on account of I saw him once in Vegas an' that's how he looked."

Welk shot him a glance of disgust. "You got me mixed up with somebody who gives a shit."

Earl Lee put down his hamburger, disbelief spreading over his fair, open features. "You jokin' me?"

"What?"

"You don't like Elvis?"

Welk didn't look at him. He took a big gulp of his Coke. "Is that supposed to be a crime or somethin'?"

"Damn straight. Elvis was the king."

"This is a democracy, my man. They's no kings."

"How come you don't like Elvis. You a Southerner. All Southerners like Elvis."

"Evidently not," Welk said.

"What's the matter with Elvis all of a sudden?"

"I just don't care for him, that's all."

Earl Lee puffed out his chest. "You just name me somebody who's better, then."

"Little Richard. Chuck Berry. Fats Domino. Lots of 'em."

"Name me one white man."

Welk glanced over at the black girl behind the counter to see if she'd heard, but she was too engrossed in her own teenage conversation to be paying any attention. "I don't see what's the difference a man's white or not whether he can sing."

"Just name me," Earl Lee demanded.

"Willie Nelson, for one."

"Willie Nelson's a damn sell-out!" Earl Lee exploded. "He didn't even pay no income tax!"

"You go to your church, I'll go to mine."

"Well, that's damn silly."

Welk shrugged. "How about Jerry Lee Lewis?"

Earl Lee slapped the table with the flat of his hand. "Jerry Lee Lewis did it with his little cousin, for God's sake!"

"That may be," Welk said, "but he could purely sing the ass off of Elvis."

Earl Lee wiped his mouth with the tiny paper napkin. "Damn, man, Elvis is what America's all about."

Welk looked at him from beneath his heavy brow. "I hope you ain't sayin' I'm not a patriotic American just 'cause I don't like the same singers you do." The threat was tacit, but it was there, and it hung between them in the silence.

"I'm not talkin' singers!" Earl Lee said, growing desperate. For some reason it was becoming very important to him to convince Welk that Elvis was the best. "I'm talkin' the King!"

Welk just shook his head and shoved a handful of fries into his mouth, then rubbed his fingers together to wipe off the salt.

"He's been dead, what, ten years now? And everybody still loves him just like he was alive. That's why they give him a postage stamp."

"A fat stamp," Welk said dismissively. "A stamp where he's old and fat."

"You don't see nobody makin' a Jerry Lee Lewis postage stamp, do you?"

"They don't make postage stamps less you're dead."

"They ain't never gonna make one for Jerry Lee."

Welk sighed. "Jerry Lee was just about the best piano player ever was," he said. "He could even play standin' up."

"I don't happen to think that's such a big deal."

"An' he wrote all his own songs, too," Welk added. "Elvis sang other people's songs. Carl Perkins and them. You think he wrote 'Blue Suede Shoes'? Elvis didn't write no 'Blue Suede Shoes.' It was Carl Perkins wrote it, an' Elvis stole it from him."

"He did not steal it!"

"I don' know what you'd call it, then."

"It wasn't stealin'. Elvis just liked the song an' covered it and he had the big hit with it 'cause he was damn well a better singer than Carl Perkins. And they ain't givin' Carl Perkins no stamp either. Thin *or* fat."

Welk made a line in the condensation on the outside of his Coke cup with a thick finger. Then he added three more lines, making it into a shiny *W* for Welk. "Don't make no difference to me one way or the other."

Humiliated, Earl Lee picked up the rest of his Whopper and chomped at it. He was taking this stranger's rejection of Elvis as a rebuff to himself, and he didn't like it one damn bit. The meat and bread stuck in his throat and he swallowed furiously, finally gulping down a mouthful of chipped ice to help wash it down. Welk ate quietly, his eyes on his tray. The swamper came closer with his mop and Earl Lee rubbed at his nose with a knuckle to counteract the smell of the disinfectant that rose like a miasma from the tile floor.

"Carl Perkins wasn't no movie star either," he said.

Welk didn't look up. The fat old swamper got to the window with his mop, made a sharp turn around the last table, and started back up the row toward them, his slack mouth moving in a song that would never be heard.

"Look at all the movies Elvis made. *Viva Las Vegas* with

Ann-Margret. *Blue Hawaii. Jailhouse Rock.*" He growled out his best Presley imitation: "Warden threw a party at the county jail . . ."

Welk didn't react.

"And how 'bout *Flaming Star*?" Earl Lee pressed on. "He didn't even sing in that one an' he was still great."

"Your opinion."

"Not just my opinion! Everybody's opinion."

Two teenaged boys came in and ordered some food, chatting up the girls at the counter while they waited. For a moment Earl Lee wanted to bring them into the argument, to ask them what they thought of Elvis, whether they didn't consider him the greatest singer and movie star ever, but then he thought better of it. They were too young, they didn't know. They'd been babies when the King died.

"Man, I don't understand you," he said softly.

Welk looked amused. "Not much reason you have to." He leaned back in his chair. "I'm not sayin' Elvis wasn't any good. At the beginning he was pretty good, I got to give you that much. But then later at the end, after he started poppin' all those pills that made him get so fat, he was nothing but a damn clown."

Earl Lee's fists were clenched so tightly that his horny fingernails dug painfully into his palms. "That's sick."

"That's what I think, too," Welk said, his dark eyes dancing. "Here's a man got the world by the short ones and he screws it all up by bein' no better'n a damn junkie off the streets. If that isn't sick, I don't know what is."

"If it's so sick how come there's millions of people that still love him? Buy his records? Rent his movies an' watch 'em over and over again?"

"No accounting for some people's taste."

"Oh, yeah?" Earl Lee took a big breath and let it out before firing his best shot. "How come most folks don't even believe that he's dead?"

Welk shrugged indifferently.

"Maybe he ain't dead, that's why."

The girls at the counter handed over several sacks to the teenaged boys, who called out loud good-byes as they walked out into the rain. Welk watched them go without much interest.

"It's true," Earl Lee pressed on. "People see him all over the place. Every week somebody sees him somewheres."

"Right," Welk said dryly. "Here's a man made twenty million bucks a year, and for the last ten years he's been hidin' out all over America, popping up at Dairy Queens. Oh, I b'lieve that, all right."

"You don't know! It could happen. He could be alive."

"Sure. An' I'm president of the United States. I just drive a big rig around all damn day an' night so's I can get in touch with the people." He looked around, exaggerating his gestures for Earl Lee's benefit. "My Secret Service guys are out takin' a leak, but they'll be in shortly for their Whoppers, too."

A flush suffused Earl Lee's face. "Well, nobody ever loved the president of the United States like they love Elvis. I got damn near every record he ever made!"

"The president?" Welk was enjoying the other man's discomfort.

"No, Elvis!" Earl Lee said with some heat. "I even got a pitcher of him, too, a painting, real nice on black velvet, hangin' right in my living room. I been to Graceland on the tour three times!"

"I could never figure out why anybody'd be willing to pay all that money just to see some rock singer's underpants."

"That's just 'cause you're ignorant!"

Welk looked up at him and something funny happened to

his face; the bones seemed to settle into a configuration strongly resembling granite. "That's gettin' a little personal, son. Don't push it." His eyes were flat, and Earl Lee knew he had crossed over an invisible line. Something hard and cold like fear formed a lump in his stomach. Or it could have just been the Whopper, settling.

The swamper came between their tables, his mop swishing within inches of Earl Lee's boots, and he pulled his feet back under his chair, looking up in annoyance. "Watch it, there!" he snapped, taking his anger out on the old man.

"Besides," Welk said, an edge in his voice that hadn't been there before. "Elvis was a fag."

As if someone had pulled an invisible plug the blood drained out of Earl Lee's cheeks. He started to say something but his throat had closed up in rage, and he coughed angrily. "That is a damn lie," he said when he found his voice.

"Is not."

"Is too!"

"Hell, everybody knows it. Always liked hangin' around with guys instead o' women. Sleepin' on silk sheets an' all. An' that fancy karate stuff instead of fightin' like a real man." His eyes glittered, flat and black like a snake's. "He wouldn't even do it with Priscilla no more. You ever see a man wouldn't do it with a fine-lookin' woman like Priscilla if he weren't a fag?"

Earl Lee squeezed the words out like pus from a suppurating wound. "He wouldn't do it with Priscilla no more after she'd give birth to little Lisa Marie because he thought motherhood was a holy thing an' he didn' wanna soil her."

The suggestion of a particularly nasty smile played at one corner of Welk's mouth. "Well, jus' let old Priscilla come around and drop her drawers for me," he said. "I'd soil her, all right."

The knuckles of Earl Lee's fists were turning white on the Formica tabletop. "You take it back," he said, low and furious like the angry hum of an alley cat.

"Won't do no such thing," Welk said. "Elvis was a pill head an' a fag an' a fat pig, an' on the best day he ever had in his life he couldn't sing better'n Jerry Lee Lewis or Willie Nelson." He pushed his tray away from him. "Now that's it, boy. I just come in here to eat a sangwich and stretch my bones. I didn't start this conversation with you, but if you wanna make sumpin' ugly out of it that's okay by me. I don' know why you care so much about Elvis Presley you wanna lose some teeth over him, but if you do I'm happy to oblige you."

"Maybe I won't be the one to lose my teeth."

Welk smiled all the way now, his eyes nearly disappearing into the deep wrinkles, giving him an almost satanic aspect. His teeth were long and crooked, stained yellow from twenty-five years of three packs a day behind the wheel. "I think you will. I been in more fights than you ever thought about, an' you wanna go around with me I'm gonna hurt you bad. I'll bite off your damn nose if I get a chance, keep you from stickin' it in other people's bidnesses. Now it's up to you. You can walk outa here or they can carry you out, don't make a bit o' difference to me. If you're smart—which I doubt, but I hope you are—you'll just sit there gettin' a hard-on thinkin' about Elvis an' finish your burger till I'm gone. If you don't, I'll surely crush you into the ground so's you'll be as dead as Elvis."

He uncoiled himself from the molded plastic chair and loomed over Earl Lee for a moment. Then he made a sound deep in his throat; it could have been a cough or a laugh. Earl Lee wasn't sure.

"You drive careful now," he said as if to a child. "It's slicker than a snake's belly out there."

He strode easily to the door, where he stopped and zipped his lightweight jacket up to the neck. The two young girls watched him fearfully. They hadn't heard any of the talk between Welk and Earl Lee, but they could spot body language a mile away and knew that whatever had gone down between the two men had not been pleasant.

They sighed with visible relief as he pushed his way through the big glass door, and shivered as a whisper of the damp breeze blew across the floor and over the counter. Then they looked at one another and giggled for a reason they couldn't really explain.

The rain had lessened to a fine mist when Hank Welk stepped out into it, and he paused in the light coming from the inside of the Burger King to fire up a Camel. He filled up his lungs and blew the smoke out through the side of his mouth.

Damn nut case, he thought. That's the trouble with driving a big rig, you meet so many nut cases. It was the solitude that did it—Welk knew it only too well. You go for hours, even days, without any human contact except for pump jockeys and little girls at fast-food stands, and something inside your head gets twisted and skewed. It was why he'd picked up on the kid's conversation in the first place, and why, when he'd found out Earl Lee was something of a loon, he'd wound up deliberately baiting him. Except for the cigarettes it was the only pleasure he'd had in two days.

He took another deep drag on the Camel and let it hang from the corner of his lips, shoving his hands into the pockets of his jacket, and started around the back of the restaurant to where he'd parked his truck.

He wasn't expecting the sharp blow to the side of his neck, delivered with the hard, stiff edge of a hand. Pain grew and unfolded like a blossom inside his head and he staggered forward a few steps, trying to get his fists out of his pockets. He turned and met a high-flying kick that shattered his jawbone and sent him reeling back against the side of the Dumpster, the coppery taste of blood filling his mouth. The next karate kick broke his sternum, and when he bounced off the metal bin another karate blow crushed his carotid artery.

He was still standing but dead even before the final blow tore his shoulder out of its socket. He crumpled against the Dumpster and was still.

Inside Earl Lee hadn't moved. Fear had paralyzed him, but the outrage more than the fear. A tear trickled down his cheek, but it wasn't for his own cowardice. Doubt burned inside him like a low flame, eating him up like battery acid. It wasn't true what Welk had said, was it? It couldn't be. Elvis was no fag, no fake, no ghost. Elvis was the best thing that ever happened to America, and in his heart of hearts Earl Lee believed he was alive somewhere, waiting to come back.

Almost like Jesus, he thought fervently.

After a moment he wiped his eyes with his napkin, crumpled it up and threw it on the tray. He got to his feet unsteadily and lurched like a drunken man to the door, not even bothering to put his trash in the container and stick his dirty tray on top. He was usually a lot more thoughtful.

As he stumbled out the door he jostled against the swamper coming in, and was about to lash out in anger until he saw the old man's eyes, deep inside pouches of fat. A look of sympathy and understanding passed between them, and then Earl Lee rushed out into the mist, hurrying to his truck without looking to the left or right. For the next two and a half hours he never took his eyes from the monotonous white line in the middle of the road.

Back inside the Burger King the swamper pushed his gray

hair out of his eyes, wiped a sheen of sweat from beneath his nose, and regarded the tile floor near the counter that he had mopped a few minutes before. Welk, Earl Lee and the two teenagers had left dirty footprints in the wetness. The old man sighed and set to mopping it again, a never-ending and monotonous task that occupied most of his waiting hours.

The two counter girls ignored him as they always did—creepy old coot anyway, they thought—so they couldn't see the small smile that played about his lips, and they talked to each other about their upcoming Saturday night plans so they couldn't hear the song he sang softly under his breath.

"Take my hand . . ." he crooned softly, almost too low for the human ear to pick up. "Take my whole life, too . . ." The spare tire of flab around his belly shook beneath his stained apron as he swiveled his hips with every swoop of the mop, and his heavy jowls almost enveloped the lower half of his face as he looked down at his work.

"Cuz I—cain't—help—fallin' in love—with—yoooooooou."

When the wonderful Charlotte McLeod read this story and I told her it was based on an event that had actually happened to me, she remarked with some amusement, "You certainly lead an interesting life."

I don't know about that. But Gore Vidal once said, "Writing comes out of living a life or having lived a life intensely." And I guess I have to cop to that one.

The genesis of this story, however, had nothing to do with the way I live. The beginning section is written pretty much the way it occurred, right through the encounter with the Los Angeles police, which in hindsight is pretty funny but wasn't the slightest bit amusing at the time.

I was luckier than Saxon, however, because in real life The Pig Man evidently tired of harassing me and went away. But then, that wouldn't have made much of a story, would it?

I lucked out a bit, too, with what the miscreant shouted, and was thus able to put an animal in the title, continuing the tradition of all my stories and novels about Saxon. This one first saw the light of day in Deadly Allies II.

The Pig Man

I make half my living involved with people you'd never ask to dinner. Punks, wise guys, skels, grifters, junkies, hookers, and the bigger, dirtier fish who feed off them. It can get sticky sometimes. Nevertheless, I don't consider myself a violent person. I cross the street to avoid confrontation, and when I do find myself hip-deep in hard guys and loaded guns, I keep kicking myself for not paying attention to my second career, which is acting. It's why I came to Los Angeles in the first place, and while no one in their right mind would call show business a kinder, gentler profession than being a private investigator, it's considerably less dangerous.

My agent had packed me off to Minnesota for a picture, which sounded okay until they had an early snow and fell behind schedule, and I wound up doing seven weeks in a town so bereft of anything to do that the locals think it's big time when they drive over to Duluth on a Saturday night and have supper at Denny's. Tends to lull one into a feeling of safety and security to spend so much time in a place where the most heinous crime they've ever heard of is crossing against the municipality's single red light.

So when I came home to Los Angeles I was ready for some excitement. I wasn't prepared for terror and sudden death.

Since my plane arrived in L.A. at nearly midnight on a Sunday, I hired a limo to ferry me from the airport to my rented house on one of the canals in Venice. Anyone who thinks you can't drive from LAX to Venice must be thinking of the city in Italy; we have one in Los Angeles too, just a few blocks from the ocean, built as a tourist attraction near the turn of the century and now home to a colorful collection of yuppies, druggies, elderly home owners who've been there thirty years, and a counter-culture stunning in its infinite variety. If you don't believe me, check out Ocean Front Walk some Sunday afternoon, where third runners-up in a Michael Jackson look-alike contest and turbaned evangelists and one-man bands on roller skates zoom past Small World Books and the endless line of stalls and shops selling sunglasses and T-shirts.

The limo was an indulgence I couldn't afford but felt I'd

earned. The back seat, the well-stocked bar, and the wrap-around sound system made me feel like a Sybarite. I like that word—like a warring tribe of ancient Judea. "And Samson rose up and slew the Sybarites . . ." Of course, Samson had not slain the Sybarites at all; they'd simply moved to Los Angeles, bought a BMW, and subscribed to *Daily Variety*.

I had invited my adopted son, Marvel, to join me in the wilds of Minnesota, but he'd turned his big brown eyes on me and said, "You got to be kidding!" So he went to stay with my best friend and my assistant, Jo Zeidler, and her husband Marsh. Jo spoils him and Marsh talks basketball to him more intelligently than I can, so Marvel didn't complain about the living arrangements.

I paid off the limo driver after we'd struggled into the bungalow together with seven weeks' worth of luggage, tipping him less lavishly than I'd planned when he observed that I must be carrying the baggage for the entire Yugoslavian army. Nobody likes a smart ass.

It was good to get home after so long, to be surrounded by my own books and paintings and furniture. And my plants. Since my lifestyle doesn't allow for pets, I'm a plant freak. I have more than fifty in varicolored pots all over the living room and about eight in my bedroom, including a ficus I'd nursed back from near-extinction and moved from my last residence in Pacific Palisades. My house sometimes resembles the set of a Tarzan movie. My next-door neighbor, Stewart Channock, had graciously consented to come in and care for the greenery while I was gone, as well as pick up and forward my mail and start my car every few days so the battery wouldn't expire.

I refuse to eat airplane food, so after dumping my bags I checked the refrigerator. Not much after seven weeks of absence—a bottle of Chardonnay, a six-pack of Guinness Stout with one missing, and a forgotten wedge of cheese that had outlived its usefulness. Nothing you could make a meal out of. What I really wanted was the kind of fancy omelet Spenser always cooks before he makes love to Susan Silverman on the living room floor—but I was out of both eggs and Susan.

Sighing, I changed into a sweatshirt and jeans and went out to my car, which by prearrangement I park across the street in the lot of an apartment building. My destination was an all-night market four blocks away. Even in the dark I could see that someone had scrawled WASH ME in the dust on the trunk, a not unreasonable request after the car had sat out in the elements for seven weeks.

I was pleased that the engine started and made a mental note to buy Stewart a bottle of scotch for his trouble. I switched on the headlights. The windshield was smeared with an overlay of greasy California grit, and which someone had written with a wet finger: **CIA**. Damn kids, I thought as I Windexed the glass with a paper towel. It's not a bad area I live in, it just ain't a great one, but then unless you're in Beverly Hills or Bel Air, there are no great neighborhoods in Los Angeles.

The next morning I called my various children, friends and lovers to announce my return, made plans to pick up Marvel that evening, walked to the corner for a *Times*, and read it out on my balcony with a mug of coffee at my side. Los Angeles doesn't have much going for it anymore except its weather; being able to read the paper outside in October is one of the few pleasures we have left.

I went into the small den I'd constructed from a storage room on the second floor of the house and booted up my computer. I'd ascertained from Jo that there was nothing pressing at the office and had decided to take a day for myself before getting back into the swing of things. I sat there

90

reading the scrolling screen. Travel fatigue made it tough, trying to get my head back into reviewing some of my old cases, including a few that I hadn't yet closed, but it beat hell out of wearing a tie, fighting the freeways, punching a time clock, and putting up with crap from a boss. We self-employed people have the best life imaginable—if we can make a living.

By three o'clock I was in high gear. Overdue bills were paid, overdue letters written, and I was feeling almost back to normal. Until something hit my window with a thump.

I work beside a sliding glass door with a peaceful view of the canal, replete with noisy ducks, an occasional rowboat or paddleboat, and every so often an empty Slurpee cup or a used condom floating by. The window overlooking the street is across the room, and when the sound made me glance over there, something wet was running down the glass. I heard a voice, raspy with hatred, scream "CIA *pig!*"

I ran to the window in time to see a battered brown Dodge van roaring around the corner as if the hounds of Hell were snapping at its tailpipe. On the sidewalk just below my window a can of Budweiser beer was still rolling.

I remembered the writing on my windshield I'd dismissed as a kid's prank, and a strange burning started in my stomach like yesterday's bratwurst sandwich. I didn't realize it then, but it was the icy heat of fear.

At six o'clock I went over to the cinder-block house next door with which mine shared a common front yard. Stewart Channock answered my knock holding a drink, wearing the dress shirt and tie in which he worked all day as a financial consultant, whatever that was. I didn't really know Stewart well; we were more neighbors than friends. We said hello in the parking lot, shared a gardener, and he'd kindly offered to water my plants while I was gone.

"Welcome home," he said. "When'd you get back?"

"Last night, late."

"Come on in. Drink?"

"I need one," I said.

He went into the kitchen and poured me more than a jigger of scotch. I swallowed it down as though I was thirsty.

"Hope I didn't kill your plants—I even talked to them. About football."

"You did a great job, Stewart. I appreciate it. Uh—when was the last time you started my car?"

He frowned, thinking. "Wednesday, I guess. Did the battery die?"

"No, no. Was anything—written on the windshield?"

"Written on the . . . ? No, why?"

I told him what I'd found and about the beer can incident that afternoon and the brown Dodge van.

He laughed.

"It's not funny," I said.

"Sure it is. Listen, the people walking the streets in this town are Looney Tunes. You start letting them get to you, you might as well go back to Wisconsin to stay."

"Minnesota. But what if this guy thinks I really am with the CIA and wants to kill me?"

"Then he would have done it, and not left his calling card. Come on, this isn't one of your movies."

Right there you could tell Stewart wasn't in show business. Actors call them pictures, directors call them films, and distributors and theater owners call them shows. No one in the business ever uses the word "movie."

"So you think I should ignore it?"

"What's your other option? Go tell the cops someone threw a beer can at you and wrote on your car, but you don't know who he is? What do you think, they're going to stake out the street and wait for him to do it again?"

I nibbled at my drink, feeling more than a little foolish. He was right, of course; I was overreacting. Seven weeks in the North Woods with nothing to do but watch haircuts, eating the Velveeta cheese which was a small-town hotel's idea of gourmet food, and living out of a suitcase takes its toll, and I was undoubtedly stretched thin.

"All right, Stewart, I'll forget it," I said, getting up. "And thanks again for the caretaking."

I went back to my own house, picking up the beer can and putting it in the big bag I take to a recycling center every few weeks. At least I'd made two and a half cents on the deal.

Jo and Marsh had invited me for dinner, and it was good to see them again. It was even better seeing Marvel. In the four years he'd been living with me I'd watched him grow from a scared, skinny adolescent who could barely read and write into a handsome, athletic and witty young man who was beginning his senior year in high school. Considering the adoption had been unplanned and almost out of necessity rather than any desire on my part to share my life with a strange black kid, it had worked out well. He'd become a part of who I am, a part I hadn't known existed, and I'd evidently done a damn good job raising him, because he was turning into a real champ.

I spent the evening recounting war stories from the trenches in Duluth, and we didn't get back home until nearly eleven, late for a school night. Marvel went to sleep and I sat up and watched Johnny and then Dave, a habit I'd fallen into on location when there wasn't anything else to do.

The next morning I was refreshed and raring to go, but my feeling of well-being evaporated like a raindrop in Death Valley when I went out to get my car and drive it to my office in Hollywood and saw someone had spray-painted **CIA** in red letters on the sidewalk with an arrow pointing to my door.

I've lived in big cities all my life, Chicago before L.A., and I've steadfastly refused to become one of those urban paranoiacs who triple-lock their doors, scan the street for possible muggers, and sleep with a .44 Magnum under their pillows which will undoubtedly discharge some day and blow off an ear. But this CIA business had me worried.

Trying to keep my mind on my work at the office was a bear. I kept worrying what might be happening at the house while I wasn't there. I decided to go home early.

I'd stopped at the store on my way home and picked up the very basics a gourmet cook like me needs to simply survive a few days—butter, garlic, tomato sauce and tomato paste, several different wedges of cheese that were not Velveeta, and milk. After changing into comfortable sweats and a pair of deck shoes with too many holes in them to wear outside, I went up to my den and sat down at my desk, reading while I ate the linguine with the sauce I'd made from scratch.

Then I heard the raspy shout from the street again. "CIA pig!"

This time I got to the window in time to see him. The Pig Man. He was over six feet tall, in his early forties with a droopy mustache, slim and ropy with a slight potbelly, long, dirty-blond hair flowing almost to his shoulders from a balding crown, in blue jeans and a turquoise muscle shirt, and just climbing into the Dodge van parked halfway down the street. The set of his shoulders was tense and rigid. As far as I knew, I'd never set eyes on him before.

He sat in the van for a moment. From my vantage point I could only see him from the neck down, his fists clenched on the steering wheel. Finally he banged them on the dashboard before starting the motor and peeling away from the curb, leaving a strip of rubber. It was profoundly disturbing. God knows there are enough people ticked off at me for good reason without having to worry about some deluded stranger.

I dumped the remainder of my lunch into the garbage disposal and poured myself a Laphroaig, neat. I never drink during the day, but I was wound as tight as a three-dollar watch. Anybody bizarre enough to throw a beer can at my window and spray-paint my sidewalk was capable of worse.

Just past three the phone rang. My agent, asking me how it had gone in Minnesota and was I interested in reading for a new series on the Fox network. I was and I wasn't; getting tied down to a six-days-a-week job didn't appeal to me, but the kind of money they pay you for a series did. I was standing in the middle of the room with the phone cradled against my shoulder, pulling yellow leaves off my schefflera plant, when I glanced out the window and saw the brown van come around the corner again and park across the street.

"I'll call you back," I said. I hung up and went to the window, being careful to stay well out of sight. The Pig Man got out, cast a look of loathing toward my house, and went into the building across the street. I waited for about two minutes, then grabbed a pencil and notepad and went downstairs to copy the number on his license plate.

I peered into the front seat of the paneled van, half expecting to see a claymore mine or a flamethrower or a box of hand grenades. All that was in evidence, however, was a crumpled Styrofoam box from Burger King and a few cans of Budweiser, one empty. That was hardly damning evidence; there must be at least a million people in Greater Los Angeles who drink Bud.

I came back inside, half expecting a bullet to smash into my back. There were twelve apartments in the building across the street, and I wondered which one he was visiting, whether its window faced mine. I usually leave my drapes open all the time so the plants can get light, but now I pulled them shut. I was as safe in my own home as I was ever going to be, and the security felt woefully inadequate.

Marvel came home and we chatted for a few minutes—it was World Series time and to my horror he was rooting for Oakland. But he had homework to do and repaired to his room, his stereo making the whole house tremble. I tried to read, but I couldn't concentrate. Instead I paced and chain-smoked, every so often sneaking a peek through the closed drapes to see if the Dodge van was still there.

It was.

Somewhere around dinnertime I heard Stewart Channock going into his house. Some human companionship would have been welcome, and I had the urge to walk next door and have a drink with him, but he would have thought it peculiar; we didn't have that close a relationship. We had nothing in common. I don't understand people who move numbers around all day long, and I was sure he was equally mystified by those who chase around after insurance cheats, embezzlers, skips, children kidnapped by divorced parents, and occasionally, people who kill.

I decided I didn't want to be in the house anymore that evening. My paranoia was going to turn me into a candidate for the rubber room if I stayed there much longer. I waited for Marvel to finish his studying and we went out to a Japanese restaurant for sushi and saki. As usual, Marvel talked up a storm, and it took my mind off my troubles.

We got home at ten o'clock, and I noted with relief that the brown van was gone. But in the living room the drapes across the window were blowing. Marvel went over to investigate and his shoes crunched on long, wicked shards of broken glass that hadn't been there when we left.

"Marvel, stay back!" I said.

He froze, looking me with eyes that were just this side of frightened. I went past him and pulled the drapes aside.

The window had been shattered, and lying on the carpet amidst the debris was a big rock. If I had been sitting by the window with the drapes open, reading, I would have been decapitated. The skin on the back of my neck tingled unpleasantly.

Enough was enough.

The next morning, slightly cranky from a hangover and from the onerous task of cleaning up the glass from my carpet, I was at the front desk of the Culver City division of the Los Angeles Police Department, talking to the desk officer, whose silver nametag said he was L. Tedescu.

I put the rock on the desk in front of him. "My name is Saxon," I said, and told him my address. "This came through my living room window last night."

He looked at it without emotion. "See who did it?"

"I wasn't home at the time."

Tedescu's eyebrows—or eyebrow, rather, he only had one that went clear across his forehead—lifted.

"I'm being harassed," I went on, and told him about the man in the brown Dodge van. "From his age and the way he was dressed, I'd guess he was probably a Vietnam veteran with a grudge against the CIA."

"*Are* you with the CIA, Mr. Saxon?"

A real rocket scientist, L. Tedescu. I felt the essence of a headache starting behind my eyes. If I didn't get at least three aspirin down my throat in the next few minutes it was going to be a bitch kitty. "First off, if I were with the CIA I wouldn't tell you. Secondly, I'd take care of it myself."

"Don't even think about taking the law into your own hands, sir," he said pompously. "You'll be the one in trouble."

"If I was going to do that I wouldn't have come here for help. I have the guy's license number." I pushed the number from my notepad across the glass-topped counter. L. Tedescu looked at it as if he could divine the mysteries of the ages from it. Then he handed it back to me. "There's not much we can do about this."

"Why not?"

"He hasn't committed any crime."

"Throwing a rock through a window isn't a crime?"

"You didn't see it. You don't know it's the same man."

"Who else could it be?"

He looked at me, his face a mask of apathy. "You'd know that better than I would, sir."

"Well, what about screaming outside my window? It scares the crap out of me."

"That may be, but it's not a crime."

"Disturbing the peace?"

He shook his head. "We'd have to arrest everyone who raised his voice. Now, if he calls you on the phone and makes threats, that's a crime. But if he does it in person it isn't, and we can't take any official action."

For a bit I was too stunned to reply. The best I could come up with was, "That's the dumbest thing I ever heard."

L. Tedescu's eyes became slits. "It's the law."

The rock sat incongruously on the desk between us. "He spray-painted the sidewalk. He wrote CIA on the city sidewalk. Defacing public property?"

"Yes it is, and he probably did it. But you didn't see him." He put his hand on the rock and moved it a few inches toward me. "Look, Mr. Saxon—right now, not five hundred yards from where we're standing, someone's probably selling illegal drugs to eight-year-olds. Armed robberies happen at gas stations and convenience marts four or five times a night in this division. People getting behind the wheel of a two thousand pound car when they're too drunk or stoned even to walk, driving up on a sidewalk and killing a kid. Rape. Spouse abuse. Child abuse. And I won't even mention the hookers and drug dealers and the knife fights in the bars."

"I understand all that . . ."

"I'm glad you do. Los Angeles just doesn't have nearly enough cops—even if what you know this guy to be doing was illegal, it'd be pretty low on our priority scale." He ran his fingers through his mouse-brown hair. "If he does anything else, if you *catch* him at it, let us know, all right? Otherwise . . ." He turned both hands palms up to show me he was powerless. "I can't even write up a report."

I glared at him for a moment, clenching my teeth to bite back all the angry, frustrated things I wanted to scream. Then I spun on my heel and stalked toward the glass doors. My righteous indignation was like a steel rod up the middle of me.

"Mr. Saxon?"

I stopped and turned back eagerly, hoping he'd change his mind and write up a report, that the police, whose motto in Los Angeles is "To Protect and Serve," would hunt down the Pig Man in the brown van so I could go on with my life and my work and not be spooked by every zephyr that stirred a tree or every stray cat prowling in a Dumpster for its dinner. "Yes, Officer?"

He held out his hand to me, and it wasn't until I got all the way back to the desk that I saw what the offering was.

"Did you want your rock?"

It's only a short walk from the police station to the sheriff's office in the Culver City municipal center. Last year's tragic murder of a young actress has made it more difficult to get someone's name and address from their automobile license plate, but nothing's impossible if you have a friend in a high place. At least I hoped she was still a friend.

Female law enforcement officers don't often look like Angie Dickinson or Stepfanie Kramer, but Sergeant Sharyl Capps came pretty close, with a headful of honey-blond hair, green eyes, and an overbite that could drive a person crazy. We'd met when I was doing a TV picture some years ago and had enjoyed a nine-week fling that ended, as most such relationships do, with a gradual distancing that eventually turned to nothing at all. She was almost as tall as I, with several medals and commendations in her service record. I wasn't sure how I would be received, but she smiled when I walked into her office—it wasn't the broadest, most welcoming smile I'd ever seen, but it was a smile nonetheless—and shook my hand in a manner that was a little too businesslike, considering.

"It's been a while," she said. The ironic lilt in her voice just made her more appealing.

"I guess it has. I've been busy."

"I know. I've seen some of your movies and TV stuff. I guess you're doing all right. Are you still a PI too?"

"Whenever anyone asks me. Sharyl, I've got a problem."

"I know." I suppose I deserved the dig. When I'd been with her I was commitment-phobic, and I guess she was still a little miffed. I winced. Then I told her about my adventures of the last few days. Her face remained passive but the amusement in her eyes annoyed hell out of me. "You're a big tough private eye," she said. "Why don't you take care of it yourself?"

"Take the needle out, Sharyl—this is serious."

"Well, the police told you right. There's not a damn thing they can do." She shrugged. "Nothing I can do, either."

I held out the paper with the license number. "You can run this for me."

She looked at it without touching it. "I'd get my butt in a sling," she said.

I thought about remarking that it would look good even in a sling, but wisely desisted. "I'm not going gunning for him," I said. "Just on television."

"Then what's the point?"

"I'd like to know who my enemy is, a least."

She started to shake her head when I said, "Sharyl, you wouldn't want my murder on your conscience, would you?"

She regarded me narrowly. "Not unless I got to do it myself," she said. She took the paper from me, pointing to a chair opposite her desk. "Park it. I'll be back in a minute."

She left me sitting there with nothing to do. Unlike dentists and lawyers, deputy sheriffs don't have backdated magazines in their offices to browse through while you wait. I did notice a framed photograph on her desk, a smiling Sharyl and a big beefy muscle-hunk, both on bicycles down by Venice Beach, looking the way southern Californians in love are supposed to.

In twenty minutes she was back.

"Who's your friend?" I said, pointing at the photo.

"He's my partner. Name's Frank Torn."

"Was that taken one day out on bicycle patrol?"

"None of your business. Look, Saxon, I've already violated procedure here. You want this stuff or not?" She waved some computer printouts at me.

I sighed. Sometimes it seems as though life is one long series of what ifs and might have beens. "Sure," I said.

"The van is registered to one Harlan Panec," she said, handing me one of the printouts. Harlan Panec lived over in

North Hollywood, in the San Fernando Valley. Not a high-rent district.

"I never heard of him."

"You sure?"

"Sharyl, if you'd ever met a guy named Harlan Panec, wouldn't you remember?"

"Just for the hell of it, I put him through the computer to see if he had a sheet," she said. "He's a naughty boy. Forty-three years old, dishonorable discharge from the army in '73, misdemeanor possession of marijuana, assault, drunk and disorderly, and several citations for speeding."

I jotted the address down in my notebook.

Sharyl frowned. "Stay away from this guy, Saxon."

I tried to be casual. "Why? He's not exactly a master criminal."

"Because." Her laser gaze reduced me to a small dust pyramid. "You're not nearly as tough as you think you are."

I called a glazier to fix the window, but of course he couldn't come for three days, so I made do with natural air conditioning and prayed for no rain. The brown van didn't appear the rest of that day, or if it did, the Pig Man didn't indulge in his penchant for screaming under windows like Brando in *A Streetcar Named Desire*, but the curiosity that was eating a hole in my gut, the twin of the one caused by fear, got to me by the next morning.

I had to see Harlan Panec, tell him he was mistaken, that he had me mixed up with somebody else, so I could get on with my life without waiting for another rock to come through my window—or worse.

The street address Sharyl Capps had given me was just off Lankershim Boulevard near Vanowen Street, a neighborhood of small industrial buildings and a few houses that were tiny, old, and dilapidated. Not many of the residents spoke English as their first language, and when I pulled my car around the corner at about eleven o'clock they were all out on the street in the sunshine, watching the black-and-white squad cars and the city ambulance, talking in Spanish or Korean or Farsi in the hushed tones reserved for the presence of death.

I pulled over to the curb and watched with them. There must have been twenty uniformed policemen running around on the barren front lawn of the house where Harlan Panec lived. The brown van was parked in the weed-choked driveway, and behind it an ancient Volkswagen Bug. On the sagging porch a woman of about forty, in baggy jeans and a tie-dyed shirt that was a holdover from the Woodstock years, was crying and screaming while a policewoman who didn't look like Angie Dickinson tried to talk to her. There were reddish-brown stains on the hysterical woman's hands and arms. It was hard to tell because emotion distorted her features, but she looked vaguely familiar to me. It took me a few minutes to remember where I'd seen her—going in and out of the apartment building across the street from me.

I got out of the car and stood near the curb as a team of paramedics wheeled a gurney out of the house and lifted it carefully down the steps. I couldn't identify its passenger because he was wrapped in a plastic bag from top to toe, but I knew in my heart it was the Pig Man I'd seen beneath my window.

"What happened?" I said to an Asian woman nearby as they loaded the body into the ambulance. She glanced at me fearfully and moved away. I wandered down the sidewalk and repeated my question to a short, muscular black man in a tank top.

"The woman come over this morning," he said, "an'

found him." He rolled his eyes and drew his finger across his throat, making a hideous sound with his mouth. "They got him in the bed."

When I got home at about one in the afternoon I poured myself a Laphroaig and downed it in two swallows. It was too good—and expensive—to gulp down like that, but sometimes need overcomes nicety. Thus fortified, I crossed the front yard, nearly tripping over a duck, and rapped on Stewart Channock's door. I'd seen his car in its space across the street, so I knew he was home. I'd known he would be anyway.

"Yes," he said, his voice muffled.

"It's me, Stewart. We have to talk."

"I'm a little busy right now." I heard him move away.

I banged on the door again, harder this time, with more authority.

"Not now," he said through the door.

"CIA pig!" I yelled. There was a pause—a loud one—and then he opened up.

We just looked at each other. Then he sighed and moved aside. "Come on in," he said.

There were two suitcases on the floor near the sofa. "Taking a trip, Stewart?"

"What do you want?"

"You know what I want. Except for a real dumb cop and a real smart lady sheriff, you were the only one who knew about the guy who was hassling me and throwing rocks through my windows. Now he's dead."

"That's got nothing to do with me."

"It's everything to do with you," I said. "The guy saw you getting out of my car last week after you'd gone over to start it for me, right? He recognized you. He must have known you from Vietnam. I happen to know he was in the army in 1973 so it figures. Then he saw you go in to water the plants and he thought it was your house."

He shrugged.

"What was it, drugs? You were involved in covert CIA drug smuggling in Asia and poor old Harlan Panec—that was his name—was in the wrong place at the wrong time and saw you."

"You have a vivid imagination, Saxon."

"A lot of guys who never got over Nam have vivid imaginations," I went on. "They came back home in the early seventies to a country that didn't give a damn, and have been fighting the war in their heads ever since, probably because they realized they'd been over there fighting for a government no better than the sleaziest drug peddler. Panec looked like he was one of them; he had that half-crazy, stretched-too-tight look. When he saw you again after all those years, the poor bastard snapped like a frayed rubber band. But he was too dumb to do anything except throw rocks and yell."

"You're talking crap you don't know anything about."

"Then pay no attention, let me ramble. Maybe you're still with the Agency, maybe not. But whatever you are doing, it's probably illegal, so when I told you about the writing on my car, the brown van, the spray painting under my window, you realized you'd been blown. You waited for the van to show up again and you followed it to Panec's place in North Hollywood and cut his throat. Probably not the first guy you ever killed."

"You'll never prove any of this, you know."

"Maybe not."

"But you're going to try?"

"I have to," I said.

He pushed himself away from the door where he'd been leaning casually. "Let's head into the bathroom, shall we?"

I shook my head. "I don't have to go."

"Move it," he said, and there was a gun in his hand. It was a small gun that fit in his palm, the kind women might carry in their purses. At close range it would kill as efficiently as a bazooka. I hesitated and he said, "Don't be stupid. You know I'll use this if I have to."

"Those are noisy little devils," I said. "People will hear."

He moved toward me. "Do you want to take the chance?"

I didn't. I don't like having guns aimed at me. I should be used to it, but I'm not. On TV, of course, the private investigator would have slapped it out of his hand and overpowered him, but it had already been pointed out to me that I'm not as tough as I think I am.

I walked into the bedroom ahead of him. Another suitcase, half full, was open on the bed. He went over to the dresser, opened a drawer, and felt around inside. Then he pulled out a pair of silvery handcuffs.

"I never knew you were into kinky sex, Stewart."

"Shut up." He motioned with the gun and I went into the bathroom with him right behind me. He switched on the light, and the exhaust fan in the ceiling began humming noisily. There were cute little aqua and black mermaids on the shower curtain.

"Kneel down on the floor by the john. Do it!"

I did it. The porcelain tile was cold on my knees through my jeans. He took my hand and fastened one of the cuffs around my wrist. "Not too tight?" he said. He put the chain around the thick pipe running from the toilet into the wall, then braceleted my other hand and snapped the cuffs shut so I was kneeling over the closed toilet as though at prayer.

"There's no window," he said, "and the fan will muffle the

noise, so don't bother yelling. Besides, no one else in the neighborhood will be home until evening."

"And by that time you're in another city with a whole new identity. Stewart, you're a slime."

"There's things you don't understand, so don't be so damned judgmental. If I was such a slime you'd be dead by now."

"You aren't going to shoot me?"

He considered it for more than a moment. Then he shook his head. "Finally you have to say 'enough' to killing." He went to the door. "You okay?"

"I'm real comfy," I said bitterly.

He looked at me for a minute. I suppose he was trying to decide whether he'd made a mistake, whether he should just shoot me in the head and be done with it. But my luck held.

"*Ciao,*" he said, and left me there.

I couldn't hear much through the closed door, but I did hear him leave the house. He was an invisible man, marching through life carrying out his own twisted agenda, and if some other poor fool like Harlan Panec got in his way, he'd take care of it the same way and disappear again, vanishing into the mist like Brigadoon. It takes a special mindset, I imagine, to live rootless without family or friends, worrying that someone was always in the shadows, watching. Not for nothing were guys like Stewart Channock known as spooks.

I shifted around on the tile floor, trying to get comfortable, and flexed the fingers of my imprisoned hands. Between the toilet and the cabinet that housed the sink was a wooden magazine rack. From my vantage point I saw two *Newsweek*s, a *Forbes*, yesterday's *Wall Street Journal*, a crossword puzzle magazine, and a couple of paperback books—but I wasn't much in the mood for reading.

I knew what would happen when I got to his car—my

making a simple phone call had ensured it—but in the completely enclosed room I could barely hear the gunshots from the parking lot, and I had no way of knowing who shot whom until Sharyl Capps and her partner/lover from the sheriff's office kicked in the door and told me.

This was my third effort for the Cat Crimes series, specifically for Feline and Famous: Cat Crimes Goes Hollywood. *When I wrote these three stories I did not have a cat. Since 1995, however, I've shared my home with a Russian blue named Sonny—christened by my son Darren after the James Caan tough-guy character from* The Godfather.

Sonny doesn't much resemble the Corleone sibling, however. While he certainly is possessed of attitude to spare, he is a lover, not a fighter, and spends most of his time while I am working either on my lap or on my mouse pad, which explains both my chronic back problems and why I don't write faster. Ironically, since becoming a cat owner, Ed Gorman and Marty Greenberg have not asked me to write another cat story.

I was once accused of never letting an opportunity go by to slam Hollywood and Los Angeles in my Saxon tales, to which I cheerfully plead guilty. My friends Robert Crais and Michael Connelly love the city and write of it with affection. I find that hard to do, since despite its justly-famed climate I find it the coldest town in the world outside of Minsk or Point Barrow. The tenor of the place is defined by the fact that, seven years after this story was written, most of the real-life movie luminaries whose names I drop have seen their careers more or less fade from public view or, in the parlance of Tinseltown, have become "toast."

This story was the final appearance in print of my Los Angeles actor/detective Saxon to date. Hollywood insiders will easily recognize the real players on whom some of the characters were based, although I will deny everything.

The Catnap

As movie sex symbols go, Eric Winslow was pretty short, about five feet eight in his ostrich-skin boots. He insisted that they cast the supporting players in his films by their height, too, so he wouldn't look Lilliputian among them, and always made sure the cameraman kept the angle low to make him appear taller. He had blond, stringy hair and a sullen, pouty mouth, and although I thought he was far too pretty to be truly sexy, there were legions of women who disagreed with me, because he commanded about ten million bucks per picture, and his projects almost always made money.

Ten mil for eight weeks of work, and he was only twenty-seven years old.

On this particular Monday morning he was wearing tight, carefully faded jeans and a plaid western shirt to match the Southwestern décor of the house, but he didn't look much like a cowboy as he wandered the Great Plains of the living room of his hacienda-in-the-hills, sucking on a mug of coffee with his own picture on it. He'd had the house built a few years before, when earth colors accented with pastels, "the Southwestern look," had been the Los Angeles trend for about fifteen minutes, up near the top of Coldwater Canyon above Beverly Hills, not too far from the estates of Marlon Brando and Jack Nicholson. I guess he thought he ought to live up there near the two movie legends because, like them, he was a star.

Not in your wildest dreams, Bunky.

Winslow's attorney and personal manager, Alexander Halliday, was watching him stare out the window at the greenish brown foliage of summer and the brownish yellow smog that hovers over the Los Angeles basin year-round, and I was watching Halliday, one of Hollywood's most prominent power brokers, who'd called and asked me to "take a meeting" because, in addition to holding a private investigator's license, I also carry a little card that says I'm a member of the Screen Actors Guild, and he thought I'd understand his client's "need for confidentiality."

But so far Winslow had offered no confidences—not much more than a mumbled hello and a dead-mackerel handshake. He hadn't offered anything, actually, and I was coveting his morning coffee. He seemed vague and distracted. For the first few minutes I thought he was on something—downers, perhaps—until I realized he was simply a space cadet.

He was even spacey on the screen. They threw him into every big-budget picture that came along, whether he was right for the part or not. He'd walked through one of the big-money revisionist westerns like Wyatt Earp on 'ludes, he'd played a hotshot young lawyer as if he'd watched too many old re-runs of *The Defenders*, and he'd even done a latter-day costume movie for which he'd learned to fence. No one was going to forget Errol Flynn because of Eric, but there was no denying the camera loved him and so, apparently, did moviegoing America.

After I'd watched him pace for a while, I raised an eyebrow at Halliday, who simply shook his head at me as an indication that I should be patient. So I waited, counting the moments of my life as they ticked by. Maybe they thought just observing America's number one box office attraction look out the window was an unrivaled treat for me.

They were wrong.

"What seems to be the problem?" I said.

Eric Winslow stopped walking and looked at me as if I'd belched in church. He ran the fingers of both hands through his too-long hair, then patted at it to make sure he hadn't spoiled the effect.

"The little bitch stole Tennis Shoes," he said.

I'd figured when Halliday called to ask me to meet with Eric Winslow that it had something to do with his highly-publicized separation from his wife of three years, Megan Evans, who was not quite as big a star as he was but was on her way. He'd divorced his first wife when he and Megan had done a picture together in Spain, and since that time they'd been Hollywood's golden couple, the darlings of the tabloids and of *Hard Copy*, their comings and goings and dinings and dancings breathlessly reported as if civilization as we knew it revolved around where they ate lunch.

For my money they were no Tracy and Hepburn, no Bogart and Bacall, not even Dick Powell and June Allyson, and it's a sad commentary on the world we live in that people give that much of a damn about two pretty and untalented people. But when their press agents had announced they were Splitsville and that Megan was going to move in with another young, hot actor, Skyler Layne, whom she'd met on her latest film, the ensuing media blitz had even knocked O.J. and Burt and Loni and Joey Buttafuoco off the front pages. Megan Evans was obviously a dangerous lady on location.

The various demands and countersuits for property division and support payments had kept America breathlessly engaged for the past two weeks, and I'd imagined that whatever investigating Winslow wanted me to do would save him a bundle. I didn't think, however, that purloined athletic footwear was important enough for him to hire a private detective. "Your wife stole your tennis shoes?" I said.

Winslow gave me the kind of contemptuous look usually reserved for those who say "him and me" at a Mensa meeting.

"Tennis Shoes is Eric's cat," Halliday explained.

Let me state up front that I don't dislike cats. I just don't own one because something in their dander makes me sneeze violently, but I have been known to admire them, especially in their kitten stage, and even pet one on occasion. I did break up a relationship once because the woman in question insisted on little Merlin spending the night snuggled between us and purring loudly enough to keep the neighbors awake, and for my money three in a bed is one too many, sneezes or no.

But on the whole I find cats engaging little creatures. I had my doubts, however, whether any cat was worth three hundred dollars a day for a PI's time. Plus expenses.

"I've had him for five years," Winslow elaborated in that slurry whine that set adolescent ganglia aquiver. "Even before I met her. He's not community property, damn it, he belongs to me. And when I came home last night he wasn't here. I want him back."

He gave his head a toss so that his hair shook out around his shoulders, a gesture I'd always associated with Veronica Lake. "Megan thinks she's so damn smart, but this is going to wreck her in the business." I didn't know if he meant leaving him was going to destroy her career, or stealing his cat, but either way he intoned it like a prophecy of Nostradamus.

"Is it possible that he got out of the house by accident and is wandering around somewhere?" I hoped not; the hills and canyons of Los Angeles are full of coyotes whose ecosystem had been displaced by the building of luxury homes, and wandering domestic pets didn't usually survive the night.

Winslow shook his head resolutely. "He never went out by himself. Not once in his whole life. He was a house kitty."

I sighed and took out my notebook. In my wildest imaginings I never believed that I would speak the next sentence in relation to a cat. "Can you describe him?" I said.

He moved across the room to a grand piano I'd bet the farm had never been played and took a framed photograph from its polished surface. "Here," he said.

Tennis Shoes, posed regally in the photo on a satin sofa cushion I recognized as the one on which I was currently sitting, was your basic garden-variety black cat with a white muzzle and four dainty white feet. Thus the name, I surmised. You can't put one over on me; that's why I get the big bucks.

"This isn't much to go on," I said. "There must be fifty thousand cats in Los Angeles that look like this."

Winslow snapped his head around to glare at me. "That's a pretty lousy thing to say."

"Take it easy, Eric," Halliday soothed.

"He'd damn well better remember who he's working for."

"At the moment I'm not working for anybody," I reminded him. "And I can live with that."

"I don't much like this guy, Alex."

"At least that levels the playing field," I said. I stood up and started for the front door, or at least where I thought the front door was. The house was so enormous, I really couldn't remember.

Alexander Halliday jumped to his feet. "Wait a minute, Mr. Saxon. I'm hiring you, not Eric. Let's not get into personalities, here. That's not the issue."

"What is the issue?"

"Getting Tennis Shoes back," Eric Winslow said. All of a sudden he sounded on the verge of tears, his eyes shiny and his little chin quivering. I guess he was really upset about Tennis Shoes, because he sure wasn't a good enough actor to make anyone think so if he wasn't.

"What about getting your wife back? Is that a possibility you'd ever consider?"

He thought about it for a while. "Sure," he said. He was easy to get along with. "If she returns my cat."

The tabloids were saying that Megan Evans had "gone into seclusion," so I figured my best starting point was with Skyler Layne. A few quick phone calls told me he was renting a house in the hills in Malibu, so I drove up there that afternoon. The traffic on the Pacific Coast Highway was as dense as it always is, and the beach homes on the ocean side of the road were built so close together that the best anyone in a moving car could hope for was a fleeting glance at the water.

As I turned up into the hills, I noted that most of the natural vegetation had been burned away by the horrendous fires of 1993, as well as several of the houses. It always amazes me that people choose to live up there; it burns out an average of once every six years.

Layne, at twenty-four, was pretty much in demand as an actor at the moment—in Hollywood we call guys like him "the flavor of the month"—but he was nowhere in the vicinity of Eric Winslow's money category, so I wasn't surprised to find that his rented house was an ordinary-looking ranch-style home with a small front lawn and a pool and sun-deck around the side, the type of home you'd find in a middle-income housing tract in one of the dreary bedroom communities that sprawled for miles east of Los Angeles. Anywhere else the place would have gone for a hundred and twenty thousand tops, but the breathtaking view it commanded of the Pacific Ocean probably upped its selling price to somewhere in the vicinity of three million bucks.

There was no sign of Megan Evans. Or of Tennis Shoes either, but then I remembered he was a house kitty.

They were all wannabes, these young actors with sullen good looks and no talent who blew in from the Midwest or from San Diego with visions of elbowing aside the true movie greats of the past and present for their little piece of the fame pie, and although I vaguely remembered seeing Skyler Layne in a film recently, I couldn't quite remember what he looked like. I wouldn't have recognized him if he'd walked up and bitten me on the ankle.

I parked in front of the house on a crushed oyster-shell driveway, got out of the car and rang the front doorbell. I didn't hear a bing-bong from inside, so I rang again, waited, shifted my feet, glanced over my shoulder at the three-million-dollar view, and tried hard to be impressed, but smog has never really been my thing.

I wasn't sure the doorbell was working, so I rapped on the thick panel with my knuckles. To my surprise the door swung open. I didn't much like the idea of that.

I stuck my head inside. "Hello? Mr. Layne?"

The only answer I got was the low hum of the air conditioner. I stepped into the tiled entry hall and took inventory.

The living room was broad and wide with a big expanse of picture window so vast that it seemed to bring indoors the well-tended half-acre of garden landscaped with exotic palms, bottlebrush and jacaranda, and some expensive statuary depicting what looked like Greek gods and goddesses in the anatomically correct nude. Inside, the carpets were green, the woodwork all blond and modern looking, the upholstery flowery. I felt as if I'd stumbled onto the set of *The Secret Garden*.

"Skyler Layne?" I called out again.

The skin on the backs of my wrists prickled, not a good sign. I wasn't carrying a weapon—I don't usually, only when I think I might need it—but there was something in the air

116

making me wish I was. I turned right and walked down the long hallway.

The first door I got to was the master bedroom. The bed had been slept in but not yet made. The covers on the left side were turned down, the sheets wrinkled, and several pillows were piled up, the top one bearing the imprint of a head. If Skyler Layne had slept here last night, he'd done so alone. I took a few steps into the room until I could see the open door of the bathroom. Except for a pair of red silk hip briefs on the floor by the shower stall, it was empty.

Under my feet something crunched—it seemed to be coarse grains of sand or stone. Skyler Layne was either a pretty good housekeeper or knew where to hire one, but whoever was responsible for cleaning up hadn't done a very thorough job on the bathroom floor.

I checked the guest room farther down the hall, but it hadn't been used recently. At the end of the corridor was a study, inexpensively paneled with a built-in entertainment center featuring a TV set about as big as the movie screen at the old Sepulveda Drive-In. The thought of Beavis and Butthead cavorting fifty-two inches across was enough to give anyone pause.

I went back down the hall, through the entryway and into the kitchen. In the sink was a mug with the MGM lion's picture on it and the dregs of coffee in the bottom, and a used cereal bowl and spoon. On the counter beside the sink was a light dusting of instant coffee crystals and an opened box of Honey Nut Cheerios. Compared to most bachelor pads inhabited by young men, this one was as sterile as an operating room.

I went back out into the living room, pulled open the sliding glass door, and went out onto the patio, the wind from the nearby coast ruffling my hair.

The breeze brought with it the faint sound of music, or at

least of an insistent rhythm, and I followed the noise around the side of the house, through a wrought-iron gate to the back. The pool shimmered aquamarine despite the perennial Malibu overcast, and I could see a padded lounge chair and a redwood table that matched the deck, on which a Diet Pepsi was drawing flies and a boom box the size of a freight car was pumping out noisy and irritating gangsta rap from Snoop Doggy Dogg.

Skyler Layne, it seemed, had already achieved a small measure of immortality, to take his place beside William Holden in *Sunset Boulevard* and Alan Ladd in *The Great Gatsby*. Like those legendary actors in their best roles, he floated face down in the pool, his body a ghastly grayish white and the blood from a fatal gunshot wound in his temple staining the water pink.

But there was no director around this time to yell "Cut."

The sun had finally pounded its way through the morning haze and was drumming down on my head and neck. I'd taken off my jacket, but there was still a damp spot on my shirt at the small of my back.

"A cat?" Los Angeles sheriff's deputy John Anger, from the Malibu substation, shook his head in deep disgust. "You mean somebody's paying you big bucks to find their cat?"

"It beats holding up convenience stores," I said, tucking the photostat of my PI license back into my wallet.

"Barely. So you came up here looking for the cat, is that what you're saying?"

"I had reason to believe it might be here, yes."

"And you're not going to tell me whose cat it is?"

"Client confidentiality. Sorry."

"You're not a lawyer," he said, "you can't claim privileged information."

"No, but I'm working for a lawyer, Alexander Halliday, and that's just as good."

"We'll check that, of course."

I shrugged. "Knock yourself out."

He squeezed out a sour little smile, but a smile nonetheless. Anger was evidently not one of those cops who thought all private investigators should be banished to an island off the coast of Madagascar. We were on the pool deck behind Layne's house watching the technicians and police photographers finish up. The solitary swimmer had been fished out of the water and taken down the hill in a body bag; all that remained was an ugly pink tinge. The pool would have to be drained.

"I don't want this turning into a media circus," Anger said. "We're trying to keep the press out of this as long as we can. So you didn't know Skyler Layne?"

"I know who he is," I said, "or was. But I'd never met him. He was renting this place, wasn't he?"

"Yeah, but don't get the idea that he was killed by mistake. The house belongs to an elderly widow who's been staying with her children in Fort Lauderdale for the last three months." He pushed his cap back on his head, revealing a startling tan line. "She lives within five hundred yards of the Pacific Ocean and she takes a vacation in Florida. Go figure."

"Any idea when he was killed?"

"We won't know until after the P.M., but from the look of him he'd only been in the water a few hours."

"If I were you, I'd try to find Megan Evans. They were engaged."

He put his fists on his hips. "I read the papers, too. But gee, thanks. You ever think about giving lectures on criminology?"

"Too busy. Right now I've got to go find a cat."

He grinned. "You're a regular one-man pussy posse, aren't you, Saxon?"

"It's a living," I said.

I drove down the hill slowly, took PCH south until I got to Santa Monica Boulevard, then turned eastward toward the towers of Venture City shimmering in the sunlight like a bad set in a science fiction movie. Artists International Agency—AIA—had their lavish and overstated offices there, and they represented Megan Evans in all her film and television dealings.

Specifically, Barbara Milkis represented Megan Evans. Revered and even feared in certain circles, Milkis had closed some of the biggest movie deals of the sixties and seventies. She retired for five years while she got out of her system a marriage to an oil tycoon who was a minority owner of a professional football team, then came roaring back in 1991, fifty pounds heavier and wrangling a new stable of viable young clients like Megan, and proceeded to rewrite her own legend.

She never missed a premiere or a SHARE benefit, was obnoxiously active in her own favorite charities like Actors and Others for Animals and AIDS research, and with the exception of her former husband, who, for all anyone knew, she hadn't been intimate with either, she'd never been linked romantically to anyone, in or out of the movie business.

Her office, on the fortieth floor of one of the Venture City towers, was arranged so that visitors had to sit very near the floor-to-ceiling window, from which they could see the ocean and Catalina Island on the rare clear day in Los Angeles, and otherwise could nervously grip the arms of their chair, as I did, hoping their incipient vertigo wouldn't kick in and make them agree to damn near anything just so they could get out of there.

And she wasn't glad to see me.

She inspected my license and then handed it back as though it had accidentally fallen into the john. "I'd never submit you for the part of a private eye," she said in a lumberjack's voice that had been carefully cultivated by twenty-five years of Marlboros and five-to-one vodka martinis at Spago. "You don't have the psychological weight."

"Don't blame me," I said, "blame Jenny Craig."

"A smart ass, huh. Well, I'm busy as hell today, so let's not mess with each other's heads, all right? I'm not going to tell you where Megan is, and I'm not going to tell the newspaper ghouls, or the police either, should they ask. The poor kid's been through hell these last few weeks. First the break-up and now this Skyler Layne thing."

"You heard about that already?"

"Jungle drums," she said. "Nobody in this town goes to pee without my knowing about it."

"I'll bear that in mind next time I drink a six-pack. Was Skyler Layne a client of yours, too?"

"Be real!" she said, scorn dripping from her tongue like maple sap in April. "He was nothing but a glorified day player. He only wanted to marry Megan because he thought it'd make him a star—but I've got a big oil painting of *that!* In two more years his career would be dead in the . . ." She stopped, but couldn't suppress her smile. "Bad choice of words, huh?"

I had to agree with her there.

"And a bad career move for Megan, too. I hope that now she comes to her senses and patches things up with Eric."

"Eric won't care that she'd been sleeping with someone else?"

"Are you kidding? Are you kidding me? Eric Winslow has jumped every loose chickie in this town—before, during and after he married Megan, so I don't think that kind of middle-class polyester thinking is going to enter into it. The man's got more notches on his gun than Billy the Kid."

"I never heard he had that kind of reputation."

She rolled her eyes. "Being a cocksman is politically incorrect these days, or hadn't you heard? His people always keep it pretty hush-hush."

I sighed. His "people." Nowadays, a star's entourage is almost as famous as the celebrity. You heard the whispered, awestruck buzz in the trendy restaurants of Beverly Hills and Malibu: "There's Tom Cruise's people," the fringe crowd will say. Or: "He's one of Cher's people."

"No wonder Megan left him," I said.

She glared at me through oversized, pink-tinted spectacles that went out of style in 1972. "What are you, some religious fanatic? You just don't divorce America's favorite studmuffin and run off with fag-bait like Skyler Layne."

"He didn't have psychological weight, either?"

She took a sip of chilled Evian water from a crystal goblet on the desk and relaxed her considerable bulk into the highbacked glove leather throne on which she conducted her business. "What's your angle in this? Why do you want Megan Evans so bad?"

"I don't. I want Eric Winslow's cat."

She started to laugh. Her whole body shook with mirth, and there was enough of it to make me worry about being up here on the fortieth floor so close to the San Andreas Fault.

Finally she caught her breath and reached under her glasses with her fingers to wipe her eyes. "Oh, dear," she said, and fanned her face with her hand. "You mean to tell me Eric is actually paying a private detective to retrieve his cat? Is that what this is all about?"

"I'm not at liberty to say."

"Then you can pound sand," she said, and made a shooing

motion with both hands. I felt like a chicken in the roadway.

I stood up, fighting off the rush of dizziness I always experience when I'm up high and trying not to look down forty stories, and put one of my business cards on her desk. "When you do talk to Megan, will you have her get in touch with me? Or," I added—a little archly, I'll admit—"have one of her people do it for her?"

Her eyes narrowed. "I certainly will," Barbara Milkis said, and with great and grave ceremony ripped the card into little pieces and tossed it into the wastebasket.

Nobody quite knows how Jackie Hatch makes his living. He lives well, in an upscale apartment just off the western edge of the Sunset Strip, and he's the confidante of everyone in town who matters, from Kevin Costner and Michael Ovitz to Jessica Tandy and Julia Roberts. He was a regular at the Bel Air Hotel for breakfast, Le Dome for lunch, and wherever there was a Beautiful People Party in the evening, and I don't think anyone in Hollywood has ever seen him pay for anything besides valet parking.

It's generally assumed he's a homosexual because his walk, speech, and gestures are effeminate, but no one has ever seen him *with* anybody, male or female. Appearing gay certainly got him to places he might not be allowed otherwise in Hollywood, because the female stars can relax with him as a male companion who isn't going to try and jump their bones, and the male stars can assume he's no threat to embarrass them publicly by taking women away from them. But for all I know, Jackie spends his spare time sitting in country-western bars in a muscle shirt, drinking Bud, arm wrestling, and spiriting a different woman into bed every night by telling them little harmless gossipy secrets about Denzel Washington and Demi Moore.

I found him at his usual cocktail-hour hangout, the Polo Lounge at the Beverly Hills Hotel. Trendy film-industry watering holes have come and gone over the last thirty-five years, but the Polo Lounge is forever. Jackie was sitting at a banquette near the door, so anyone entering couldn't possibly miss him, and he couldn't miss them. There was a white telephone on his table, right next to the champagne cocktail.

"Well, if it isn't the shamus-to-the-stars," he called out when he saw me, waving a languid hand in greeting. "Are you here to buy me a drink?"

I slid into the banquette beside him. "I'm here to trade you a drink."

His eyebrows arched. "For what?"

"Some information."

He idly fingered the ascot he was wearing in lieu of a necktie. "Information costs more than a drink in his town," he said. It's funny how people who live here always refer to Los Angeles, or at least to the non-geographic but specific psychological boundaries of Hollywood, as "this town." Often there's a rude modifier just after "this."

"Doesn't that depend on the information?"

He glanced at his Rolex. "I wouldn't tell you what time it is for less than a hundred."

"Maybe I have some information I can trade you, then."

He laughed. "I doubt that."

The cocktail waitress came over. She was gorgeous, much prettier than most beauty contest winners, and about twenty times as sensual. I ordered my favorite Scotch, Laphroaig. It's a single-malt with a smoky, peaty taste that they only serve in the best places. Like the Polo Lounge.

"On the rocks?" she said. Well, maybe they don't serve that much of it.

"Neat, please—in a snifter."

Jackie pointed to his own drink and nodded, and the young woman went away to fill our order and dream of the day when she'd have made it, when she'd be drinking a Polo Lounge champagne cocktail instead of serving it.

"What I have for you is primo, Jackie."

He leaned back in the banquette and crossed his arms across his chest, a sardonic smile twisting up one corner of his mouth. "Skyler Layne was found floating in his pool with a gunshot wound to his head at about noon, and you were the one who discovered the body," he recited.

I was a little taken aback. "I'm impressed," I said. "How did you find out?"

"I knew it three minutes after you called the authorities in Malibu. Was that your primo bombshell?"

" 'Fraid so."

He snickered, savoring his little triumph.

"You're a hard man, Jackie," I said. I took a wad of money out of my pocket—I always carry it loosely in there rather than in a wallet or money clip—and counted out five twenties and pushed them toward him. What the hell, I was on expenses; it was Eric Winslow's money anyway, and a hundred dollars to him was like a nickel to everyone else. Less, even.

Jackie didn't touch the money. "What's this for?"

"The whereabouts of Megan Evans."

He looked at me with some amusement.

"She walked out on Eric Winslow and no one has seen her since. Everybody's got to be somewhere, Jackie."

He flicked at the bills with a polished fingernail. "Divorcing the biggest star in Hollywood to marry a guy who was snuffed less than eight hours ago, this wouldn't buy you a wad of her used Kleenex."

"Suit yourself," I said. I raked the money toward me and stuffed it into my shirt pocket, and I couldn't miss the sudden flicker of panic in his eyes. He started to say something when Miss Gorgeous arrived with the drinks on a tray, bending over a trifle more than was absolutely necessary when she put them on the table; for all she knew, I was an important producer or agent.

Jackie took his and swallowed half of it. "You won't find out anywhere else," he warned.

"Sure I will. I'm a detective, remember?"

"Yes, but my sources are impeccable. You know that."

"I'll find your sources, then, whoever they are, and save myself a few bucks—eliminate the middle man."

He ran his fingers up and down the stem of his glass in a gesture that can only be described as masturbatory. "Well," he said, licking his lips, "since we're old friends . . ."

I took the money out of my pocket and he snatched it away, his hand as quick as the strike of a rattlesnake.

"London," he said.

"Megan is in London?"

"At a little inn just outside, actually."

"How long has she been there?"

"Since she walked out on Eric. She's there under another name, and probably wearing a dark wig. She wants to lay low from the press until the tumult of the separation dies down." He shook his head sadly. "Bad move. It's going to hurt her with the great unwashed moviegoing public, mark my word."

"Are you sure she's in London?"

"Be serious," he said scornfully. "My source is unimpeachable."

"Who's your source?"

"If I told you that," he said, "you might give the next hundred to him." He took another sip of champagne, a smaller one now that he wasn't agitated anymore. "Now you can tell me something."

"It'll cost you a hundred bucks."

He laughed. "Oh, it's not worth nearly that. Just my idle curiosity, that's all. Why do you want to find Megan Evans?"

"I don't," I said. "I'm looking for her cat."

The laughter evaporated like morning dew on an August afternoon, and his expression turned pettish. "Fine, don't tell me," he snapped. He slid out from beneath the table, stepped down from the little banquette and stood looking at me, hands on top of his butt, fingers pointing toward the floor. He'd been taller sitting down.

"You're a queer duck, Saxon," he said.

"Look who's talking."

After he left I finished my drink at leisure; Laphroaig is too good—and too expensive—to chugalug, even if you're in a hurry.

Miss Gorgeous came by with the bill, giving me another scenic view of her cleavage along with a sizzling smile. If she'd known I was an out-of-work actor and a part-time private investigator, she probably would have made a paper airplane out of it and flown it over from the bar.

The amount of the check surprised me, so I ran my finger down the items listed there. They included three champagne cocktails from before I'd arrived, as well as the drinks Jackie and I had together. I wondered who would have picked up the tab if I hadn't come in.

Somebody would have. That's just the way it works, even at the Beverly Hills Hotel.

I ransomed my car from the valet. It took a while because it was a Chevy Corsica, and they only park the Rolls-Royces and Mercedeses and Ferrari Testarossas up front where anyone can see them. I drove east on Sunset, winding past the mansions whose annual tax assessments would feed a family of four for ten years, then hit the Strip, and finally wound up in Hollywood proper, heading toward my office on Ivar Avenue just a block and a half from Hollywood and Vine, a corner fabled in folklore but now, in the nineties, about as glamorous as the boy's locker room in a junior high school.

The office was dark save for the desk lamp in my inner sanctum. My assistant, Jo Zeidler, had gone home already, but she'd left my phone messages in the middle of my blotter along with a typed note:

ALEX HALLIDAY PHONED FOUR TIMES BETWEEN 1 O'CLOCK AND 5. HE'S HYSTERICAL. CALL HIM BACK SOONEST.

J.

XOXOXOX

Jo was as fond of capital letters for emphasis as she was of kisses and hugs, although she saved the real ones for her husband Marshall, a waiter in a Westwood restaurant and screenwriter manqué.

I have my own bottle of Laphroaig stashed in a standing metal supplies cabinet—sorry, the bottom drawer of the desk is full of my pictures and resumes. I poured a stiff shot into a cardboard coffee cup, but it didn't taste as good as the one in the Polo Lounge. Then I sat down and called Halliday.

"Jesus Christ, where've you been?" he said, and on the last word his voice soared up into that rarified altitude where only the dogs can hear.

"Looking for your cat," I said.

"Who gives a damn about the cat anymore?" he said. "The police were at Eric's house all afternoon. They had a search warrant and everything. Don't you realize he's looking at a murder rap?"

"Did he do it?"

128

There was a pause, and I could hear him breathing. He sounded a little wounded. "What an absurd idea!"

"Wronged husband, crime of passion, grieving cat lover. No jury would convict him. Don't worry, he'll skate."

"You aren't funny."

That hurt. I always thought I was.

"You've got to find out who killed Skyler Layne."

"I don't investigate murders, Mr. Halliday. The police do that, and they take a dim view of private investigators getting under their feet. I could lose my license."

"Eric could lose his career."

A man had been shot in the head and left floating in his swimming pool like a fallen eucalyptus leaf—but trust a Hollywood power player like Alexander Halliday to keep his priorities straight.

"You find Layne's killer and get Eric Winslow off the hook, I'll pay you anything you want," he said.

"You still want me to look for the cat, too?" I said, but for an answer I got a dead telephone line.

I hung up and took a pull on my single-malt. After the third sip I didn't even notice the taste of the cardboard.

Megan Evans had been in London for the past two weeks, Jackie Hatch had said, and if so, her passport would verify that. So she wasn't on my short list of Skyler Lane's probable slayers. Besides, as far as I knew, she didn't have a motive. She loved the guy. Enough to walk out on a ten-million-dollar-per-picture meal ticket.

Eric Winslow, on the other hand, had a great reason for wanting his competition dead. In addition to the normal anger over loss of consort that a jilted husband might feel, there was his ego to consider. With movie actors you always have to factor in the ego. Here he is, the biggest box office star in the world, and his gorgeous young wife walks out on him for a nobody. He was probably brooding up there in his *faux* hacienda that everyone would think he was lousy in the sack—and for a sex symbol that's pretty much the kiss of death.

And movie stars like Winslow, who are accustomed to having tough guys fall at their feet with one punch, often tend to confuse the characters they play with reality.

I was liking him for the killing and feeling good about it for about fifteen minutes until it started bothering me that he'd hired me to chase down his missing cat. Not something one is likely to do on the same morning he'd taken a human life. And I'd been with Winslow at ten o'clock, and watched enviously as he drank his coffee and didn't offer me any. It was possible he'd been out at the crack of dawn to do some killing, but not likely.

My next thoughts were of Alexander Halliday. But although he might be angry with Skyler Layne for stealing Megan away from his client, killing him seemed a trifle extreme. And he'd been there at Winslow's house that morning, too.

Of course, any one of the three of them might have hired it done—but I didn't think so.

By the time I finished my drink it was seven o'clock and I'd done a good bit of thinking. I put the bottle away, made a few phone calls, and then headed back west. The sun was a huge orange ball burning a permanent image onto my eyeballs.

The house was on the flatland just south of Sunset, the so-called low-rent district of Beverly Hills, even though the homes there sold for around eight hundred thousand, six hundred of which was just so you could boast of a Beverly Hills address. On such fine points of social status was Hollywood run. I parked at the curb and walked up the flagstone path to ring the doorbell. The chimes inside sounded like Big

Ben, and from around the side of the house I heard the throaty bark of a large dog, at least as big as a golden retriever.

Barbara Milkis answered the door with a martini glass in one hand and a leather-bound script under her arm. She'd switched from her office power suit to a voluminous flowing garment that used to be called a muumuu when it was popular thirty years ago. She was surprised to see me. Stunned, even.

"What the hell do you want?" she said.

"Tennis Shoes."

She cocked an eyebrow. "Are you collecting for the Good Will now?"

"That's very amusing, Ms. Milkis. But we both know that Tennis Shoes is Eric Winslow's cat."

"I don't have him."

"Are you going to invite me in?"

"No, I'm not, since I don't have the cat. Or did you come for something else, too?"

"You never know," I told her, and squeezed past her, not an easy task since her bulk just about filled up the doorway.

Her entry hall was atrium-style, with a skylight and about twenty huge potted palms and tropical plants. I kept looking around for Stewart Granger to step out of the bush in his safari suit.

"You have a lot of balls forcing your way in here."

"See? I have more psychological weight than you thought."

"You also have one minute to state your business and get out of here."

"For starters, I'll take the cat. And if you don't hand him over, Eric Winslow will swear out an arrest warrant. For—catnapping, I guess."

She put the wine glass and the script down on a marble

table and leaned against the jamb of the open door. "Megan took the cat when she moved out. It's with her—wherever she is."

"I don't think so," I said. "Megan is in London, and it so happens that England has a six-month quarantine on pets. She'd hardly have taken the animal with her."

Her eyes turned down at the corners when I mentioned London. "Pretty good, Saxon. All right, so I have the cat. Megan dropped him off here on her way to the airport. If it's important enough for you to barge into my home, I'll give him to you." She pushed herself off the door and started for the sweeping staircase. "Satisfied?"

"Not entirely. Because Megan didn't leave the cat with you, she left it with Skyler Lane."

She posed at the bottom of the staircase, head thrown back. The kind of thing Joan Crawford might have done—if Crawford had weighed two hundred and fifty pounds.

"Stefan!" she called loudly, and after a few seconds I heard a door open toward the back of the house. Then a tall, muscular blond man came out of the kitchen in white shirt-sleeves, a plain black tie, and dark pants. An iron-pumper, from the look of him. I figured he was her driver—they never call them chauffeurs in Hollywood anymore unless they wear livery and drive a limousine. He was about thirty, and had ice-blue eyes and one of those tight mouths you just know is going to speak with some sort of accent.

"Stefan," Milkis said, "would you show Mr. Saxon out, please?" Since I was standing about ten feet from the door, even Stefan couldn't have missed her meaning.

The blue eyes turned on me, even more icy than before, and he took a step toward me. I thought I could probably take him, but I didn't feel like trying.

"I wouldn't, Stefan," I said. I didn't give him a reason, but something in the way I said it made him think about it a little. He stopped halfway between me and his employer.

"All right, so I got the cat from Layne's," Milkis snapped. "After I talked to you I figured the poor little thing was scared to death up there, and there was nobody to feed him, so I went up and got him and brought him home here. Is that a crime or something?"

"As a matter of fact, it is—crossing a police line and violating a crime scene. But that's not what happened."

"No?"

"No. Because I walked through Layne's house before I found his body, and there was no Tennis Shoes anywhere."

"He was probably hiding under a bed."

"Did he take his litter box with him?"

"What?"

"I went into Layne's bathroom. There were little grains of sand and gravel on the floor, just like cat litter—but there was no box."

She pushed a strand of hair out of her face and looked over at Stefan.

"I think you killed Skyler Layne," I said. "You knew that if Megan left Eric Winslow for Skyler, her career would be ruined. I heard that all over town—including from you. And you just couldn't stand the thought of all that potential money slipping through the cracks—or the scandal, which might taint your other clients. So you figured with Layne out of the way, you could make Megan come to her senses and go back to Eric, who's a much bigger star and could do her some good."

"You ought to be writing screenplays," she murmured.

"But your grand passion is animal rights, isn't it, Barbara? And you couldn't stand the thought of that poor little cat starving to death up there with no one to feed it—so you brought it home with you, and the litter box, too."

She motioned to Stefan, and suddenly there was a little .22 handgun in his meaty paw. It glistened silver in the light.

"I guess I had one detail wrong," I said, raising my hands away from my body so Stefan wouldn't get itchy. "You had your driver do it all for you." I pointed. "You'd think he'd have been smart enough to get rid of the murder weapon."

"But you won't be around to tell anybody," she said. "Stefan, take him somewhere and get rid of him."

Through the open door we all watched as three cars pulled up. One was a sheriff's vehicle, and the other two were from the Beverly Hills Police Department. Contrary to popular belief, the BHPD does not drive Lamborghinis.

"I took the liberty of telling someone already," I said, indicating the cars. "And Stefan, I'd put that thing away if I were you. If they walk in and see you with a gun in your hand, they'll just surely blow you away."

It was Deputy Anger who finally found Tennis Shoes, cowering under a bed in one of the upstairs guest rooms. He was one of those limp, hanging cats that simply relaxed every muscle when picked up, as sullen and detached as his owner, Eric Winslow.

He seemed to like me all right, though. He curled up on my lap and purred contentedly in the car, while I sneezed violently all the way up the hill into Coldwater Canyon.

I had more fun with this one than anything else I've written since my mystery fiction career began. I spent many years as a TV writer in Hollywood, most of my work being in the comedy field, and I was delighted to have the opportunity to write something genuinely funny again.

The assignment—for the anthology Once Upon A Crime— *was to take a fairy tale written by The Brothers Grimm and turn it into a crime story.*

When I checked the complete tales out of the library I was shocked to find how very violent they were, most of them a lot closer in spirit to "Reservoir Dogs" than to "Babar the Elephant." My enjoyment of those stories when I was a kid probably explains why I grew up to write the kind of stuff I do.

In the Grimm's "The Brave Little Tailor," the title character annihilates seven flies that have landed on his bread and jam with one swat. When he makes himself a sash that reads "SEVEN AT ONE BLOW", the simple villagers (why were the villagers always simple in the old days? No TV or Internet, I suppose) assume he's referring to seven men and commission the poor fool to whack a couple of marauding giants. I guess giants didn't have the NFL or the NBA back in those days and had to take their aggression out somewhere—and where better than on the heads of those simple villagers?

At any rate, I updated the story to present-day Manhattan and gave it a few twists for laughs, and acknowledge a debt to Damon Runyon, whose style I unconsciously aped. To William Shakespeare, some of whose lines I shamelessly cribbed, and to the old Danny Kaye film, The Court Jester, *written by Melvin Frank and Norman Panama.*

I read this story aloud to about a hundred workshoppers at the Wildacres Writers Conference in North Carolina where I taught for several summers, and when I was done (the audience response made me realize I'd been funnier than I thought I was), a woman rushed up to me, squeezed my hand, told me she was a lesbian, and thanked me profusely for writing something in which a gay person turned out to be a strong, capable hero. Of course that was not particularly my intent, but it made me realize how often readers approach a writer's work with their own agenda and find hidden meanings and messages the author didn't even know were there.

So if you want to read it that way, be my guest. But what I'd really like you to do is laugh.

The Brave Little Costume Designer

Oliver Jardiniere left his job in the wardrobe room of the Martin Beck Theatre at ten-thirty that evening with a spring in his step that was almost a skip. It may be argued that Oliver walked that way all the time, but tonight was special. Having agonized over suitable outfits for the seven dancing chorus boys in the new Broadway musical he was costuming, tonight he had come up with a single design, varying only in color and fabric, that would do for all of them. It would save him long hours making sketches and sewing and doing trial-and-error fittings, and perhaps most important, it would stop the seven of them from buzzing all over his costume shop like rapacious flies, begging and entreating and demanding.

He'd now completed all the designs for the show, and the creative part of the job was done. He felt a little sad and let down on top of his elation. Finishing a show was almost like leaving home for the first time.

He turned toward the river on West Fifty-third Street toward the little spaghetti joint where he'd arranged to meet his current companion, Lot, for a late supper. Thinking of Lot, Oliver's walk slowed just a tad, for the relationship wasn't going well. It wasn't going well at all. It wasn't Lot's fault, really—it was simply that the magic was gone.

Once inside the restaurant, with dinner and wine ordered, Oliver breathlessly told Lot, who had suffered through the past week's aborted designs and discarded ideas with him, the happy news.

"I did it! I actually did it! I took care of all seven of them at one time," he said. "Bing-bing-bing-bing-bing!" And he made a pistol of his thumb and forefinger.

At the booth against the wall, Guglielmo "Little Guggie" Mazzarino, a loyal soldier in the army of Big Caesar Annunziato from Red Hook, tore his attention from the well-displayed cleavage of his dinner companion, one Debbie Marie Positano of West Forty-eighth Street in the neighborhood that was once called, for good reason, Hell's Kitchen, and took note of Oliver Jardiniere and what he was saying. Oliver was speaking so loudly and enthusiastically that Little Guggie couldn't help overhearing, and since he was uniquely familiar with the "bing-bing-bing" concept—and he didn't use his forefinger, either—he eavesdropped with undisguised interest.

Lot was excited for his roommate. "I don't believe it!" he said in a hushed tone.

"It wasn't that hard. I just kind of—sneaked up on them, and—"

"My God, you have the guts of a burglar!" Lot enthused.

Little Guggie Mazzarino, straining to listen, leaned sideways toward the two men like a listing ship just before it sinks beneath the waves.

"It didn't take any guts," Oliver said. "The way to do it

came to me all of a sudden, and I just went ahead and did it without worrying over it. Now those bastards won't ever bother me again." He and Lot tinked glasses as the stuffed-shells-with-pesto arrived.

At the next table Little Guggie frowned. Had something gone down tonight that he didn't know about? If so, his employer, Big Caesar Annunziato, would be righteously pissed. And that was a consummation devoutly to be avoided. Little Guggie removed Ms. Positano's stockinged foot from where it rested in his crotch, went to the pay phone in the back of the restaurant, not being high enough up in the food chain to rate his own cellular, and called Big Caesar.

He was told that, indeed, on that very evening seven members of the rival DiGiralamo family had met with some misadventure in a warehouse down on the docks, involving a good deal of semi-automatic weapons fire engineered by a person or persons unknown, and when he informed Big Caesar that he believed the person or persons was at this moment slurping pesto sauce at Mama Angelina's, he was assured that if he knew what was good for him he would bring said person forthwith to the Annunziato compound in Red Hook, Brooklyn.

And so it was that Oliver Jardiniere, Broadway costume maven, was entreated and coerced into leaving Lot in the middle of his tiramisu and accompanying Little Guggie from Mama Angelina's restaurant, his napkin still tucked under his chin like a bib. He was hustled into Little Guggie's black Oldsmobile Sierra and escorted to the home of Big Caesar Annunziato, where he was presented to the mob boss like a gift to the Christ Child.

Big Caesar was unimpressed at first, and suspicious of strangers. "I never seen you before," he gargled.

"We probably travel in different circles," Oliver explained.

"Where you come from?"

Since Oliver was always loath to tell people he hailed from Pierre, South Dakota—especially since when he pronounced it correctly, "Peer," nobody knew what in hell he was talking about—he named the place he'd lived for three years, working at the Flamingo Hotel, before coming to New York and cracking the big time.

"I'm from Las Vegas," he said.

"Vegas? What's your name?"

He wasn't about to admit that his name was really Albert Gardner—he had left that one in the dust of Pierre. Instead he said, "My friends call me Ollie."

Big Caesar sat up a little bit straighter in his chair. This must be the infamous Ollie the Ox—in the somewhat narrow world of gangdom legend, a creature of nightmare, who was likely to turn up in Chicago one week, Miami the next, then Cleveland or Detroit—do his appointed deeds with discretion and dispatch, and disappear before anyone left standing knew he'd been there. And no one in any of the New York five families had ever seen him before.

Big Caesar could taste the canary feathers in his mouth.

But he couldn't let on; he had to play it tough, cool, careful, as though he didn't know he was talking to one of the foremost freelance enforcers in mobdom. "Vegas, huh? And you think you can just come walkin' in here on my turf and be the big shot, the big swingin' dick?"

Oliver pulled modestly at a forelock. "I've never had any complaints before," he offered.

Big Caesar and Little Guggie exchanged significant looks. An unknown shooter from Vegas could come in mighty handy for what Big Caesar had been turning over in his mind for months.

"You want to do a job for me?" he said, straightening his black bow tie. Big Caesar loved tuxedos—it was his wont to

139

wear them on a nightly basis, even when he was staying home. And on this particular evening he was surrounded by four extremely attractive chorus girls, as was also his wont, late of the dancing ensemble of the most recent Broadway revival of *Guys and Dolls*, in which Big Caesar was a substantial, albeit silent investor. So Oliver can be forgiven for thinking he was a producer.

"Well—I just finished with my last job tonight. Why not?"

Oliver's very matter-of-factness about dispatching seven souls to the Big Trattoria in the sky sent chills up Big Caesar's hairy back. He was a cool one, Big Caesar'd give him that. And he talked funny. Walked funny, too. Like no one Big Caesar had ever known. But with the dispatch of seven major players in the DiGiralamo family, a unique opportunity was presenting itself—and Caesar had survived and prospered by taking advantage of such unique opportunities.

If he could somehow eliminate the heads of the DiGiralamo and Pingitore families without becoming implicated himself, he, Big Caesar, could step in and fill the leadership vacuum.

"You come back here tomorrow night, nine o'clock, and I'll tell you all about it," he said. "And to show you my heart's in the right place . . ." He peeled ten bills off a roll and handed them to Oliver, who didn't realize they were hundreds until he got home and put them in a place Lot would never dream of looking, at the back of the vanity drawer where Oliver kept his daintiest underthings.

At nine o'clock the next night he presented himself to Big Caesar once more.

"Vinnie 'the Fox' DiGiralamo and Pasquale 'the Bull' Pingitore," Big Caesar intoned.

"Yes?"

"I want you should take care of them. You know—like you did those seven guys last night."

Oliver didn't know how Big Caesar had found out about his brilliant seven-for-one costume coup, but his own producer, Irving Shlepkowitz, had been thrilled not only with the concept but also with the substantial savings it entailed, and Oliver supposed that all producers had some sort of network through which they shared information, and that Irving had probably bragged to his producing colleague, Big Caesar, of the skill and cunning of his costume designer.

"Can I see a script?" he said. "I need a script, don't I? I can't just work in the dark."

"Improvise," Big Caesar suggested.

"All right, but that just makes it harder. Where can I find them?"

"They'll be at the Ristorante Palermo on MacDougal Street."

"Oh, God, the *Village!*" Oliver protested. "It's so tacky anymore, so unsoigné."

When Big Caesar seemed unmoved, Oliver sighed a deep sigh. "Well, if I must, then. What kind of a budget are we talking about?"

"That's good," Big Caesar said. "A man like you wants to talk business first, I respect that." He went to his safe and pulled out three thick packets of bills bound in rubber bands. "There's thirty large here," he said, handing them over. "Do a good job. Nice and clean. And fast."

Oliver rolled his eyes ceilingward; producers were all the same. "Do you want it *fast?*" he said in the time-honored whine of creative artists everywhere, "or do you want it *good?*"

He didn't wait for an answer; the questions were rhetorical.

He took a cab from Red Hook to the Village, oblivious to the conversation his cab driver attempted to engage him in about something mysteriously called the Nix. As in, "How 'bout the Nix?" or "You think the Nix got a chance this year?" Oliver had heard other New Yorkers speak of the Nix, but since he didn't know what it was, he declined to discuss it. He was too busy thinking about his most recent commission.

If Big Caesar was willing to spend thirty thousand dollars on just two costumes for Vinnie the Fox and Pasquale the Bull, what must the budget be for the entire show? Visions of tulle and ostrich plumes and shimmering metallic Mylar danced in Oliver's head.

He arrived at the Ristorante Palermo to find Vinnie the Fox and Pasquale the Bull in deep conversation in a back booth. Several large, uncouth-looking men rose to deny him access to them, but when he mentioned Big Caesar's name, like a magic password in a fairy tale, all resistance melted away. Big Caesar, Oliver thought, must be a very important producer, and he wondered idly why he'd never heard of him before.

One look told him that Pasquale the Bull, whose napkin, tucked under his chin, was stained with marinara sauce and a Valpolicella of an indifferent vintage, was going to be impossible. He was short and squat and must have weighed more than three hundred pounds, all of it gut, and he had a shiny bald pate to boot. He would look positively horrendous onstage, like a hippo in rut. Hopeless, Oliver thought, unless . . .

Think black, Oliver said to himself, something long and flowing like a caftan or a djellaba in billowing silk. Think vertical stripes. Think platform heels.

Vinnie the Fox, however, was another story entirely—and it was a love story, at that. Vinnie the Fox was aptly named—

tall, possessing the chiseled features of a young Tyrone Power, black wavy hair with an errant curl that fell across his forehead and made him appear vulnerable and in need of protection. Oliver was swept off his feet at first look, into a magical world full of glitter and soft-focus clouds and show tunes playing softly in the background.

This was it. The Big One. Big casino. Thoughts of Lot, and of the former soulmate, William, who had dumped him for a performance artist–art choreographer, were banished. Oliver was smitten, truly smitten, for the first time in his life.

Almost ignoring Pasquale the Bull Pingitore, he locked gazes with Vinnie the Fox, his own blue eyes sending laser messages into the soulful brown ones of the object of his desire. He swooped, he fluttered, he flirted shamelessly, he flattered Vinnie on his breadth of shoulder, slimness of waist, depth of chest, his coloring, the way he carried his head, despite Vinnie's glossy suit that made him look like a refugee from a Martin Scorcese film, and his too-thin and undistinguished gray tie. In his head he envisioned Vinnie in a suit of ecru linen, nipped at the waist and flared at the hips to emphasize the gladiator-like physique, worn over a creamy lemon shirt, a solid mocha tie that would bring out Vinnie the Fox's eyes, a chocolate-brown Borsalino worn at a rakish angle over the forehead with ostrich-leather shoes dyed to match—Oliver would begin haunting fabric shops and specialty men's stores first thing in the morning. And then he fantasized the two of them in a large, exquisitely furnished penthouse with huge, slanted windows overlooking the lights of the East River, picturing himself slowly removing each item to eventually reveal the Olympian god beneath.

Vinnie DiGiralamo was a little overwhelmed. The scion of one of the five-state-area's oldest crime families and one of the most dedicated womanizers on the Eastern Seaboard, he was more than used to being fussed over. But Oliver Jardiniere's attentions were new to him, and while they made him more than a little uncomfortable, the fulsome praise worked its way with him, and he found himself beaming in the sunshine of Oliver's adoration.

Pasquale the Bull, on the other hand, felt his irritation mounting, until he could taste for the second time the highly spiced sauce that had covered the fettuccine noodles of his recently eaten dinner. It wasn't as if he had any illusions about himself; his mirror told him every morning that he was a squat, ugly toad of a man. He simply resented having the fact pointed out to him, especially in front of his rival Vinnie the Fox, and soldiers from both their families. It was humiliating, and showed a lack of respect, and while Pasquale the Bull was noted for his habitual perspicacity, discretion, and even temper, the one thing he could not and would not abide was any disrespect to his person, his position, or his family. He signaled the waiter to bring another bottle of the Valpolicella, and when it arrived, he sent it back to the kitchen in a fit of pique, pronouncing it cat piss.

Oliver extracted a promise from Vinnie to meet him at noon the next day for luncheon and a fitting in his small West Side studio. He would have to move slowly, he thought, and carefully. This was no fling to Oliver, it was the beginning of a lifetime of caring and sharing, and he didn't want to spoil things by coming on too strong. And there was the matter of Lot, of course, and of extricating himself from what had become a most unsatisfying liaison.

Then, remembering his commission from his producer, Big Caesar, he offhandedly assured Pasquale the Bull that he would be calling him for a fitting as well, and flowed out the door of the Ristorante Palermo into the night, his senses reeling happily, his libido simmering, his heart a veritable dancer inside his slim, frail chest.

"Big Caesar has some strange friends all of a sudden," Pasquale observed when the door had closed behind Oliver. He spoke quietly, but a flush of anger suffused his simian features.

"I thought he was very nice," Vinnie answered.

"He thought you were nice, too. I think he wants to do you."

"Excuse me?"

"He wants to do the job on you."

"Meaning no disrespect, Pasquale the Bull, but I think you're probably full of shit."

"All I'm saying is, the guy was coming on to you, and you were eating it like it was your mother's *salsiccia*."

"I hope, Pasquale, that you are meaning no disrespect to my mother, who, as you know, passed on three years ago. I hope, too, that what you are saying is not that I am the type of person which walks a little light in his loafers."

"All what I am saying, Vinnie, meaning no disrespect, is that you were certainly acting like a person which believes in fairies."

"I think, Pasquale, that you are meaning a lot of disrespect," Vinnie said, and upon the word he rose from his seat, pulled out his Sig-Sauer automatic, and blew a large hole right where Pasquale the Bull's eyebrows came together over the bridge of his nose.

At another table, Pasquale's twin cousins, Mongo and Mario, and his nephew Severio, upon observing Vinnie the Fox's ill-considered action, rose as one and cut Vinnie almost in half with fire from their .357 Magnums. This caused several members of the DiGiralamo contingent in a booth across the restaurant, already nervous and on edge because of the slaughter of seven of their compadres in a waterfront warehouse the previous evening, to stand up and fire their weapons as well.

The guns roared like thunder, a total of fifty-three times, and when it was all over, eight men lay dead on the floor of the Ristorante Palermo, leaving the establishment's proprietor-chef, Paolo Bacciagalupe, wringing his hands and wondering (a) who was going to clean up the mess, (b) who would pay for the broken dishes and the repair of the bullet holes in the walls, and (c) what in hell he was going to tell the cops when they arrived.

Noon of the following day arrived and departed, leaving Oliver heartsick and disillusioned. The cucumber-and-watercress sandwiches he had prepared so lovingly, even cutting the crusts off himself, the Earl Grey tea, the one red rose in a slender bud vase on the tray had all gone for naught. It became obvious that Vinnie the Fox had stood him up.

He could have at least called, Oliver sniffed. And after he'd gone home from the Ristorante Palermo and told Lot that he'd have to move out by the end of the week, too.

With slumping shoulders and heavy heart, he was clearing away what would have been a romantic luncheon, when the door to his studio was flung open and Big Caesar Annunziato came bursting in, followed by Little Guggie Mazzarino and two chorus girls whom Oliver had actually seen before but didn't recognize without their stage makeup and cat drag.

"What a guy!" Big Caesar enthused, taking Oliver's face between his two meaty hands and kissing him on the mouth. "What a guy! Not only Vinnie and Pasquale, but their soldiers, too. A genius!" he said, kissing Oliver again. Then he lowered his voice to a more respectful tone. "No, not a genius. An *artist!* Didn't I say that this morning as soon as I heard, Guggie? What'd I say?"

"You said 'an artist,' Big Caesar," Little Guggie parroted.

"But I didn't even do anything yet," Oliver protested.

"Listen to this guy, will you? Modest on top of it. Lemme tell you a little secret, Ollie. In this world, you gotta toot your own flute, otherwise nobody's gonna toot it for you."

As Oliver pondered the physical improbability of tooting his own flute and the depressing possibility that no one would do it for him, Big Caesar took his face between his mitts again and squeezed his cheeks, causing his lips to pucker like Tweety Pie's in the cartoons.

"Whatsa matter? You look like you lost your best friend."

Oliver considered telling him, but decided Big Caesar might not be the person who would give him the most sympathetic hearing. "I'm depressed," he said. "It's a—relationship thing."

"Hey, hey, hey! Shine it! There's a million more where that one came from, especially for a guy like you."

At that moment a brilliant thought fired the synapses in Big Caesar's brain, lighting them up like one of the pinball machines the profits from which in all the five boroughs and Connecticut found their way into Big Caesar's pockets. It was even a better idea than the one he'd had to wipe out Vinnie the Fox and Pasquale the Bull in one fell swoop.

As with most men who share Big Caesar's ethnicity, the idea of family, of royal succession, was vitally important to him. And yet the good Lord had never seen fit to bless him and his wife with a male child, or even a nephew, to whom he could someday pass on the mantle of *capo di tutti capi,* boss of bosses. All he had in the way of issue was one daughter, Benita, who was named for Big Caesar's own personal hero, Il Duce, the former dictator of Italy, and who, being something of a nymphomaniac, was singularly ill-suited to run the Annunziato family when Big Caesar finally met his reward.

And yet there was this empire he had created—dope and police and gambling and prostitution, to say nothing of the seafood importing company that laundered all the money he made off the rest—that would surely pass out of the Annunziato family for lack of male succession, just as the throne of England had slipped through the fingers of the Tudors upon the death of Henry VIII.

Big Caesar's idea, which had begun as a tiny speck, grew bigger and bigger inside his head until it threatened to explode.

"Ollie," he said, almost unable to contain his glee, "I want you should come to the house tonight for dinner. Seven o'clock."

"Sharp," Little Guggie added. When Big Caesar was around, Little Guggie always tried to act the tough guy.

So it was that at seven o'clock sharp, Oliver Jardiniere stepped out of a taxi in front of the Annunziato house in Red Hook. He was admitted through the wrought-iron gate and subjected to a full-body frisk by two of Big Caesar's employees, a process he rather enjoyed, and was then ushered into the dining room, where he found Big Caesar with a proud arm around his daughter, Benita.

Benita didn't want to be there at all—for two reasons. The first was that she would have much preferred spending her evening with Sean Malone, a young dockworker who had a shock of red hair and a face that might have come right out of the Book of Kells, and who was the latest in a long line of inappropriate young men whose brains Benita was boffing out. The second was, her father had informed her with undue emphasis that this night she was to meet the man he wanted her to marry.

Oliver wasn't bad-looking at all, Benita decided—if you like the effete, willowy type, which she did not. But like everyone else in Brooklyn, and most of Manhattan and Queens as well, she knew better than to cross Big Caesar once he'd set his mind to something.

The dinner was a work of art, the centerpiece of which was a seafood risotto cooked by Paolo Bacciagalupe, who was working as Big Caesar's personal chef while his own restaurant in the Village was shut down for repairs and a thorough cleaning. The wine flowed as freely as Big Caesar's praise of Oliver; he was trying hard to "sell" Benita on the idea of marrying the young man and keeping the family business within the family.

When the plate of biscotti and pastilles was down to mere crumbs, Big Caesar expansively suggested that the two young people "go for a nice walk or something" to get better acquainted. Oliver, who was feeling stuffed, thought a walk would settle his dinner, and agreed.

So he and Benita, followed at a discreet distance by Little Guggie and two more of Big Caesar's handpicked janissaries, strolled the streets of Red Hook in the orange gloaming. Since the warmth of the day had faded along with the sunshine, Benita had donned a cape she'd bought at Bloomie's and a gray snap-brim fedora that had once belonged to her father. She thought she looked pretty sharp.

"You're awfully quiet," she said after they'd walked a few blocks. "Is anything wrong?"

"I hate who does your hats," Oliver said.

"What's wrong with my hat?"

"It looks like something Humphrey Bogart left behind on the set after they'd finished principal photography on *The Maltese Falcon*," he replied. "I see you in something softer, something that will bring out the symmetry of your pretty face and highlight your hair. A beret, perhaps, for casual wear, and one of those little Peter Pan hats with a feather for when you go out in the evening. And the cape—the cape has to go. Why hide that beautiful figure under a shapeless cape? Tell you what—first thing in the morning I'll do some sketches for you, and we can look at them and you can decide."

Benita's heart melted. Growing up motherless in the Annunziato family, surrounded by Big Caesar's hitters and shooters and button men, she had never before met a male who had a lick of fashion sense. She decided then and there to put herself into Oliver's capable hands for a total makeover. From then on, the two were inseparable. Oliver realized that, for reasons he knew not of, he had fallen into some high, fragrant clover.

Three months later they were married before the altar at St. Rocco's Church in Red Hook, with Benita resplendent in a bridal gown Oliver had designed and sewn especially for her. Everyone from the Annunziato side of the family agreed they'd never seen a more beautiful—or tastefully dressed—bride.

Immediately after the ceremony and the reception, which yielded more cash-stuffed envelopes than Oliver had ever seen before, the happy couple flew to St. Bart's for their honeymoon, a wedding gift from Benita's father.

On the bridal night, Benita emerged demurely from the bathroom of their hotel suite clad in a black bustier, matching garter belt and hose, and a pair of crotchless panties, an ensemble that, in her single days, had never failed to make Sean Malone go ballistic. But to her astonishment, her bridegroom remained unimpressed.

To move things along a bit, Benita stretched out on the bed next to him and told him in no uncertain terms exactly what she wanted him to do to her. He reacted in a fashion that, to her, was very surprising.

"Who'd want to do *that?*" Oliver said, crinkling his nose in distaste, and rolled over and went to sleep.

After two solid weeks of this, it finally dawned on Mrs. Benita Annunziata Jardiniere exactly what was wrong. Upon their return to New York, where they took up residence in a penthouse in an upper Fifth Avenue co-op that normally refused to admit theater people, Catholics, or anyone whose surname ended in a vowel until Big Caesar made the screening committee an offer they couldn't refuse, Benita took a taxi all the way out to Red Hook and told her father of her disappointment.

Big Caesar raged. He stormed. He bellowed. He shouted and stomped and put his fist through the glass of a faux Louis Quatorze breakfront he'd ordered several years earlier for the dining room. Not knowing where to direct his anger and mortification at having been fooled, having lost face, having been disrespected by a man to whom he'd not only deeded his hard-won empire but also to whom he'd given his only child, a man who apparently regularly committed that sin we dare not name, he fired the housekeeper, old Mrs. Sidotti, who had been with the family for thirty-six years. He had his cat, Serafina, put to sleep. It was only after Little Guggie begged and entreated and invoked the name of the Blessed Mother herself that he was dissuaded from having the legs of Monsignor LaRussa, who had performed the wedding ceremony, broken in several places.

He bade Benita go upstairs to her old room, which still had several dolls and stuffed animals on the bed and a poster of Billy Idol affixed to the wall with Scotch tape. Then Caesar, raging for revenge with Ate by his side come hot from hell, took the BMT to Manhattan by himself—the first time in twenty-four years he had gone out of his house alone. He transferred to an uptown subway, got off at Columbus Circle, and hailed a cab, which took him across Central Park to the co-op where Oliver awaited him, all innocence.

"Dad!" Oliver said when he answered the door, and threw open his arms for an embrace. Instead, Big Caesar punched him right in the mouth, sending him stumbling backward across the Aubusson rug, banging into a Queen Anne end table, and sending a Tiffany lamp crashing to the floor in pieces.

As Oliver sat there, his back against the sofa, gently fingering his bloody lip, Big Caesar proceeded to tell him exactly what he thought of him, calling him every bad name in the book and a few that weren't even in there.

"You made a monkey outta me, Nancy-boy," he rumbled. "And nobody makes a monkey outta Big Caesar Annunziato."

Upon the word, Big Caesar slowly put his hand inside his jacket for the automatic pistol with which he'd vowed to send Oliver to hell. His movements were tantalizingly deliberate and precise, because he wanted Oliver to feel the fear, to sweat and plead and beg before he blew him away.

But Oliver was faster. Reaching under his silk caftan, which he'd made for himself with some material left over from a production of *La Cage aux Folles* he'd costumed at a dinner theater in New Jersey, he pulled out his own .22 pistol, which he had carried ever since three gay-bashing hooligans beat him up coming out of a leather bar in Tribeca several months before. With it, he shot Big Caesar in the throat, some eight inches lower than he'd hoped. Big Caesar staggered, fell, and died gurgling.

Then Oliver stanched the bleeding of his lip, dressed himself in one of the twelve Armani suits he'd purchased with the bounty paid him for Vinnie the Fox and Pasquale the Bull, called down for the doorman to summon him a taxi, and went out to Red Hook to reclaim his bride and to announce to the soldiers and underbosses and *capos* of the Annunziato family that, like Alexander Haig when Ronald Reagan was shot, he was in charge.

The marriage, I am happy to report, worked. Benita, who had never held much fondness for her father anyway, became known in gangland circles as the best-dressed mob wife in history, and since her husband didn't care one way or the other, resumed her affair with Sean Malone, and subsequently with a string of Sean Malone clones.

Oliver ran Big Caesar's crime family with a firm but gentle hand. He outlawed jeweled stickpins and pinkie rings for all his employees, and insisted rather forcefully that from now on they buy their clothes at Brooks Brothers. Instead of sleazy nightclubs in Brooklyn that featured pomaded Italian boy singers warbling "Chena Luna," once a week he took his most trusted lieutenants, foremost of whom was Little Guggie Mazzarino, to dinner at someplace elegant such as Le Cirque and Twenty One, and thence to the theater, usually to see a musical. After two years, Little Guggie knew all the lyrics to every song Stephen Sondheim ever wrote.

Since he had quickly gotten over the loss of Vinnie DiGiralamo, Oliver had no qualms about constructing a discreet relationship with one Sonny Donofrio, the beautiful young man who had served as the undertaker's assistant at Big Caesar's funeral. They remained together for seventeen years.

And since he'd never been Ollie the Ox in the first place, Oliver became known throughout the underworld—and at One Police Plaza as well—as Ollie the Gent.

And so the little designer lived like a king all his lifetime.

When Carolyn Wheat asked me to do a story for her Murder on Route 66 *anthology, I was momentarily stumped. I was born and raised in Chicago, where the old Route 66 began, and lived in Los Angeles, where it ended, for many years. But I figured, rightly, that there were authors now living in those cities who would take them for their own. My current home, Cleveland, is nowhere near the old highway.*

I chose St. Louis, simply because it was one city I had visited several times recently and knew well enough to write about.

I don't suppose the plot is new—no plot really is. But I know there are many predators out there who truly believe that because of their status and education and bank balances, their lives are more important and worthwhile than other people's. This short story gave me the chance to explore that chilling mindset.

Willing to Work

Meacham Donalson snaked the big white Caddy along Gravois Avenue, Alternate U.S. Route 66, in the heavy lunch-hour traffic, taking the air conditioner's blast directly on his face. It almost numbed his fingers on the wheel, but the high temperatures of the St. Louis summer made turning it off and opening the windows unthinkable. It was one of those muggy days when the moisture-laden air coming off the Mississippi was almost thick enough to drink.

Meacham glanced through the tinted window at the pedestrians on the sidewalk and sighed. He'd miss St. Louis, despite the heat, miss the majestic rumbling river even though the city had turned its back on it and moved its core several blocks west. He'd miss the Cardinals the most, he thought, even though it wasn't the same anymore now that his boyhood heroes, Musial and Marty Marion and "Country" Slaughter and Red Schoendeinst had faded. St. Louis was a pretty good town to live in, despite the heat and humidity, and even if it weren't, after thirty-six years you get used to a place, to its shops and restaurants, to its pulse and rhythms.

St. Louis had come back from economic troubles; they were saying the whole country's economy was coming back after the recession of the late 1950s, the pundits on the OpEd pages of the *Post-Dispatch* and John Cameron Swayze on NBC. Tell that to all the people in the cities who were still out of work and foraging in garbage receptacles to feed their families.

It was that damn Bobby Troup song Nat King Cole made so popular that had brought them in—kids from downstate Illinois proudly wearing their good-conduct medals and combat infantryman badges, farm boys from little towns in Missouri and Oklahoma, all wanting to "go through St. Louis" after the war to get urbanized and healthy in the wallet. It had worked that way for a while in the postwar prosperity boom, and then reality had set in.

Meacham saw them on the streets now, lined up for a cot and a square meal at one of the many shelters that had sprung up around the city in church basements or abandoned storefronts, or huddled over trash-can fires in the wintertime, living on the riverbank and willing to do just about anything for a buck.

But one man's troubles were another's good fortune.

Meacham Donalson would do anything for a buck, too,

but Fate had smiled on him when she'd assigned his birth to a well-off couple, his father in the investment banking business with a nice house in Clayton. Meacham had drifted into that world too, but it was every bit as distasteful to him as what the unemployed were willing to do—day work on construction gangs or hiring themselves out to homeowners who had tree stumps to pull or rocks to haul, or the small businessmen who needed temporary help and saw the cadre of the out-of-work as inexpensive and off-the-books muscle. Investment banking just paid better, that's all.

But not well enough for Meacham. A hundred K a year wasn't worth the aggravation, the blinding stress headaches and the mainlining of aspirin, the three martinis at the end of the day just to untie the psychological knots.

But that world was all behind Meacham now, or it would be after today. Right in the pocket of his suit jacket he had the airline ticket to Mexico, to a little place on the Baja Coast that no one had ever heard of called Puerto Vallarta. He had the phony passport with his new name, for which he'd paid a whopping two thousand dollars to a counterfeiter in Chicago. He'd made the deposit on the big white villa overlooking the coastline. And he'd sworn he'd never again put on a tie and wing tip shoes and toady to a well-heeled account, never again feel the crunch in his gut when a stock price dipped or a mutual fund went belly-up.

No, his worries were almost over. Two million dollars plus would go a hell of a long way in an obscure, sleepy fishing village like Puerto Vallarta.

He'd left work early, claiming he wasn't feeling well, that he'd been having dizzy spells for two days and thought he was coming down with the Asian flu. The people in the office had been very solicitous, had even offered advice from the current best-seller, *Folk Medicine*, on how to take care of himself;

when it comes to someone else's health, everyone thinks he's a doctor.

But he'd told them he was already taking medication. And when he'd walked out of the brokerage firm with his briefcase in his hand, he'd been amazed to realize there wasn't a single person he was going to miss. Not his boss, certainly, not the other account executives, not the women in the typing pool, not even the office boys with whom he'd discuss the fortunes of the Cardinals each morning by the coffee machine.

He was getting away clean.

He cruised downtown for about an hour, comforted by the rumble of the Caddy's big V-8 engine, sweating beneath the sunglasses with their heavy black plastic rims. He glanced off-handedly at the pedestrians, because he was looking for one particular guy, someone he'd seen on the streets several times before, the one who'd sparked his great idea in the first place.

Finally, in the depressed area known as Dogtown, he spotted him.

He was about Meacham's age and height, a tall man in an army surplus jacket and worn Levis, and a red Cardinals' cap which looked like it had been through a decade of baseball seasons. As Meacham had seen him so many other days of this long, sweltering summer, he was standing at the curb with a bulging duffel at his feet and a hopeful expression on his face. In front of his chest he held a large sheet of gray cardboard, on which had been scrawled, **NEED MONEY, WILLING TO WORK**.

Meacham slowed the Caddy to a stop, leaned across the seat and rolled down the passenger-side window. There was a fluttering in his stomach he'd never experienced before, and he coughed to clear an unexpected frog from his throat. "Hi there," he said.

The man stooped down so he could see into the car. He

hadn't shaved in several days, and the collar of his shirt was frayed ragged, but he seemed clean.

"I've got some work I need done," Meacham said pleasantly. "Stuff I need moved from the spare room to the basement. Books and things—heavy. I'd do it myself, but I've got a bad back." The man hesitated. "Take you two hours, maybe a little more."

"Sounds okay," the ragged man said, his eyebrows twin arches of hope. "Uhhh . . . ?"

"Twenty dollars, plus lunch," Meacham told him. "If you don't mind the drive out to Frontenac."

Stunned, the man blinked rapidly when he heard the amount; in 1960 twenty dollars was a fortune. "Sure. I guess so."

"Get in, then."

The man opened the car door, putting his hand-lettered sign in the back seat. He slid in beside Meacham, hugging the small duffel to his chest as if it were a child. "I really appreciate this," he said. His speech was more refined than Meacham had imagined; perhaps this was an educated man down on his luck. "Appreciate the chance to work."

"Hey, I help you out, you help me out. That's the way the world operates." Meacham leaned across him to roll up the window again and was aware of the man's odor. He smelled almost dusty; it wasn't acrid or unpleasant, but it was an odor nonetheless. Meacham left the window open a crack at the top.

"My name's Chuck," the man said.

"Mine's . . . Mike." Meacham used the name that was on his false passport; he'd spent the last ten days getting used to it. He took a pack of Old Golds from his pocket and offered one to Chuck, took one for himself, and punched in the Caddy's electric lighter.

It took him a few minutes to get back to Route 66. By the time they were rolling along nicely in the westbound traffic flow, Chuck had told him that he'd been laid off from the Budweiser plant more than a year ago, that his unemployment benefits had run out and he'd gone through his meager savings, that he'd been on the streets for about four months now, trying to find a job and a place to live and picking up small change by offering himself for whatever kind of odd jobs he could get there on the street corner in Dogtown.

"That's too bad," Meacham said, trying to make it sound solicitous and caring. "Wife? Kids?"

Chuck shook his head. "No, thank God. It's bad enough to be on my uppers like this without having to worry about feeding a family, too."

As the car picked up speed, the smoke from their cigarettes was sucked out through the top of the open window by the slipstream. Meacham dropped the visor down to block the glare of the high summer sun. The guy didn't sound like a moron. He didn't talk like a Ph.D. either, but he seemed as if he had a brain or two in his head. Meacham had a momentary twinge of remorse, and almost changed his mind about what he was going to do. But he shook the feeling off like a dog shaking water from its coat. He steeled himself. It was too important to his future.

When they finally got to Frontenac, Chuck gazed out the car window at the pristine houses, the well-manicured lawns bright green despite the summer-long drought, the tree-shaded streets. "Nice," he said softly, but there was no trace of envy in it. Longing, perhaps, but no envy. He'd been on the street four months now; he was already beyond that.

The Caddy turned into a blacktop driveway sloping up a small rise to a six-year-old ranch-style house painted off-white with a tan trim. The door of the detached garage rose smoothly like a stage curtain as Meacham activated his automatic opener and steered the Caddy in next to a battered black 1952 Buick Roadmaster with a big gouge in the paint on the right-hand door.

"Here we are," he said, and cut the motor.

They crossed the small yard to the back door of the house, went in past a washer and dryer in the utility room and into a spacious kitchen with a breakfast nook tucked into a sunny bay of windows. Except for a mug in the sink with the dregs of breakfast coffee in the bottom, the kitchen was spotless. Through an archway Chuck could see a formal dining room, and beyond that a tasteful living room all done in antiques with expensive period furniture. There were two brass kerosene-burning hurricane lamps on the mantel for decoration, another on the drum table next to the sofa.

"My wife's been gone for a week, now," Meacham explained. "Visiting her sister in New York. You know, shopping and shows." He stopped for a moment, aware that referring to a luxury vacation in front of a man who begged on the street had been insensitive. But then he shrugged off the guilt—what did it really matter?

"I wish I could've gone with her, but I couldn't take the time off from work. Still, I like to keep the place as neat as she does. I don't like clutter in my life." He put down his briefcase, took off his suit jacket and draped it over one of the chairs in the breakfast nook, and loosened his tie. The central air conditioner was on **LOW** and it was still warm in the kitchen.

"You're probably hungry, right?" Meacham said. "You want something to eat before you start? A sandwich?"

Chuck put his duffel down in one corner of the kitchen. "Uh . . . sure. If it isn't too much trouble."

"No trouble, no trouble at all. That was part of the deal. Take a seat, relax a minute."

Chuck sat down in the breakfast nook and watched while Meacham got out some Wonder Bread, mayonnaise, a jar of pickles, and some sliced chicken wrapped in delicatessen paper and began building a sandwich. He put it all on a plate, took a paper napkin from a holder, a knife and fork from the drawer, and set everything on the table in front of Chuck.

"How 'bout a beer to go with it?"

Chuck nodded, a little stunned. He hadn't expected all this, lunch and chitchat, and it was making him a trifle nervous. He'd been plucked off the sidewalk for work before—it was how he'd survived the last four months—but in every other case his temporary employer had treated him pretty much like a non-person, speaking to him only enough to explain what the job required. No one had ever offered him lunch and a beer before. He stared out the window at the well-kept pachysandra lawn and the beds of iris and crocus marking off the borders of the backyard as his host busied himself at the refrigerator. He heard the hiss as the cap of a beer bottle was popped, and turned his attention back to Meacham.

"What do you do, flop at one of the shelters downtown?" Meacham asked over his shoulder.

"Whenever I can." Chuck applied mayonnaise to one slice of bread, replaced it, and carefully cut the sandwich in half. "There aren't ever enough beds, and you can only stay there three days in a row. Sometimes I sleep down on the riverbank, when the weather's nice, or down under the Eades Bridge."

"That's rough. But you've got to keep hoping. I'll bet your troubles are going to be over pretty soon." Meacham brought a pilsner glass with a Budweiser already poured and set it next to Chuck's plate. "There you go," he said. He sat down opposite Chuck, leaning forward on his elbows, his white cuffs gleaming. "Go on, drink up. You can have another one if you want."

Chuck lifted the glass in a kind of grateful toast and took a long swallow. It was stinging cold, bitter but good, the first beer he'd tasted in more than a month. He didn't want to appear too interested in the drink so he set it down and bit into the sandwich, shaking off the uneasy suspicion that Meacham was watching him a bit too closely.

"How many boxes do you have?" he asked after he'd chewed the first mouthful of chicken.

"Boxes?"

"You said you had boxes you wanted moved to the cellar."

"Oh. Yes. About thirty, I think. I didn't really count them. But they're heavy suckers—books, papers, things like that. And my back has a way of going out every time I lift anything heavier than my briefcase."

"You should exercise," Chuck said.

"Who has the time? They've got me crazy at the office. I don't have time to do any of the things I want to do. But that's going to change." Meacham nodded grimly. "Pretty damn quick now, that's going to change." He seemed to be talking more to himself than his visitor.

Perspiring heavily under his jacket, Chuck drank some more beer to cool himself off. It was so good and cold, it made him a trifle giddy. Perhaps he just wasn't used to drinking anymore, he thought, or maybe it was because he hadn't had anything to eat for the past twenty-four hours. The alcohol burned pleasantly in his stomach.

"You mind if I smoke?" Meacham asked. "While you're eating, I mean?"

"Hell, buddy, it's your house."

"Mike. Call me Mike, okay?" Meacham waited expectantly. All at once, it seemed terribly important that Chuck call him Mike, his new name.

"Mike," Chuck said slowly.

Meacham smiled—it was the first time he'd heard it aloud. He took out an Old Gold and lit it with his Zippo. "Want one?"

"When I finish eating."

"Well, feel free." Meacham pushed the pack across the table at him. Chuck just bobbed his head in gratitude and finished the beer.

"Here, let me get you another one." Meacham almost snatched the glass from his hand and took it back to the refrigerator.

"This is really nice of you," Chuck said.

"I'm just glad I can help. I help you out, you help me out, that's the way it works. I won't insult you by saying you've got it easy, because I know you don't." Meacham had his back to Chuck, pouring the beer at the refrigerator. "It must be pure hell, not having a place to live. But for people with jobs— sometimes the rat race gets you down, you know?" He turned and came back to the breakfast nook, handing the full glass to his guest. "Cheers," he said, and took a slug of beer straight from the frosty bottle as Chuck tilted the glass to his lips. "Things. You break your back trying to keep your head above water just so you can have things. Wanting things becomes so important to you, you can hardly think of anything else." He sat back down again. "How's the sandwich?"

"Great," Chuck said, putting the glass down. His tongue was starting to feel a little thick, his lips rubbery, and he was becoming uncomfortably warm. "Mind if I take my jacket off?"

"Be comfortable."

He hung the jacket over the back of his chair. The blue

work shirt was faded and its cuffs were beginning to ravel, and he rolled them up to just below his elbows so Meacham wouldn't see. Half-moons of sweat circled his armpits and his shirt was wet at the small of his back.

"Yeah," Meacham was saying, "they hit you with a million bills every month. House payments, car payments, this payment, that payment. Insurance." He shook his head sadly. "That one's a bear, life insurance."

Chuck nodded. He was sleepy all of a sudden. He just wanted to close his eyes, and he had to struggle to keep them open.

"But it's worth it. My insurance premiums would choke a horse, but if I died, my wife would get a cool million. Tax-free. Doesn't seem fair, does it?"

Chuck was going to shake his head, but it seemed too heavy for the effort. Meacham's voice sounded as if it were coming from a long, dark tunnel.

"And if I died accidentally—that's double indemnity and she'd get two million. Think about that for a while."

Chuck tried to think about it, but he couldn't. He wasn't able to think about much of anything anymore, just about going to sleep.

"But," Meacham added, "if the insurance company only thought I died—why then I could have my cake and eat it, too. Know what I mean, Chuck?"

Chuck didn't say anything; he couldn't. The drug that had been slipped into the beer had practically paralyzed him. He began rocking from side to side, like Ray Charles, fighting desperately for equilibrium. Finally a black liquid wave flowed over his eyes and brain, and he lost consciousness and slipped off the chair onto the floor of the breakfast nook.

Meacham Donalson stayed very still for a moment, not

even daring to breathe. Finally he exhaled softly, carefully. "Chuck?" he almost whispered.

There was, of course, no answer; he hadn't expected one. The two men were motionless, like statues, once because he couldn't move and the other because he didn't dare to.

Finally Meacham stood, pushing his chair back into place. He knelt and took Chuck's limp wrist in his hand to feel for a pulse. It was there, faint but racing.

He slipped his arms under Chuck's, clasping him around the chest. Carefully he dragged him through the dining room and living room, down the hallway and into the master bedroom, Chuck's heels leaving twin trails in the thick-pile carpeting. Meacham felt a twinge in his lower back from pulling such a heavy weight while stooped over, and thought it would be the supreme irony if this did give him back problems, something he'd never suffered from in his life.

Panting from the exertion, he left Chuck on the floor of the bedroom for a moment. Maybe Chuck was right, maybe he *should* exercise. He sat on the edge of the queen-sized bed, girding himself for the next step, which he wasn't relishing. He watched the man's chest rise and fall in a lazy rhythm.

His energy finally returned to him, and he set to work. He stripped off all of Chuck's clothing, grunting as he slipped the trousers from the inert body, handling the gray underwear and badly mended socks with some distaste, stuffing it all into a plastic grocery sack from the A & P.

He looked down at the nude form, the pale, unhealthy-looking skin beneath the somewhat sunburned face and neck. About what Meacham had expected, given the man's insufficient diet and his prolonged exposure to the elements. Chuck had evidently spent the previous night in a shelter, because he had recently showered; his hands, feet and body were clean.

Meacham then took off his own clothes, every stitch, laying them casually on the bed. He went to his closet, taking down a garment bag full of clothing—a blue shirt, khaki slacks, a lightweight gray sports jacket, blue socks, and a belt—all brand new. No one had ever seen him wearing them before. He put on fresh underwear and donned everything from the bag except the jacket, and slipped his feet into a pair of Florsheim loafers he'd purchased the week before.

Checking himself in the mirror, he smiled with satisfaction. He always looked more youthful when he was wearing casual clothes, he thought, and vowed that once he got to Puerto Vallarta he'd never put on a suit and tie again.

He dressed the unconscious Chuck in the clothes he'd just taken off, all except for the tie, which he tossed carelessly on the floor next to the bed, and the shoes. Meacham was known for his fastidiousness; leaving his suit jacket on the chair in the kitchen and his tie on the floor would reinforce the fact that he had been ill at work and suffered dizziness. It was only logical that he'd go home and lie down immediately.

He left his wallet in the hip pocket of his trousers so they'd find it on Chuck. There was nothing in there he'd ever need again—his wife Bettyann would still have her credit cards when she joined him in a few months.

He took the grocery sack containing Chuck's clothes back into the kitchen, stuffing them into the man's duffel and then taking it out to the battered Roadmaster in the garage next to his Cadillac. He'd seen the car on the street in one of St. Louis' black neighborhoods with a FOR SALE sign in its window, and had bought it for cash, four hundred dollars, from an elderly man who seemed amazed he didn't haggle about the price. The car was a piece of crap, needing a new transmission and God knew what else, but that didn't much matter. It ran, and it didn't have to take him very far. He'd driven it into the garage a few days earlier, at three o'clock in the morning, and nobody knew it was there.

He went back into the kitchen and put away the lunch fixings, washed Chuck's dishes and beer glass, and placed them back where they belonged. He tossed the two empty beer bottles into the garbage, being careful to rinse the fingerprints off them first. He also wiped down the surface of the table in the breakfast nook. Not that anyone would bother lifting fingerprints, but one couldn't be too careful.

With the vacuum cleaner he went over the carpet thoroughly, obliterating the heel marks from when he'd dragged Chuck through the house. Satisfied, he stored it in its usual place in the utility room, winding the cord around the handle the way Bettyann always did.

He returned to the bedroom where Chuck still snoozed on the floor, and hoisted him onto the bed, on top of the spread with his head on the pillow. He opened the bedroom window and nodded in satisfaction when he felt the warm breeze outside circulating throughout the room. Then he went into the bathroom and opened that window, too, creating a nice cross draft. He took a small bottle of pills from the medicine cabinet, the ones he'd had Dr. Stein prescribe for him over the phone the day before when he'd called up and complained of flu-like symptoms. There were sixteen pills in there, to be taken four times a day until used up. Shaking all but three of them into his palm, he went back into the bedroom and put the bottle on the nightstand with the cap off. Then he wrapped the rest of them in a tissue and put them in his shirt pocket.

He put on his new jacket and thought for a long while, one finger playing idly with his lower lip. Chuck hadn't gone anywhere in the house except the kitchen, and Meacham had cleaned that up pretty well. The bedroom looked about right, too. He'd covered all the bases, he thought.

His guest was snoring softly on the bed, but Meacham rolled him over on his side and the sounds stopped. He arranged Chuck's right hand outflung. Then, sucking in a deep breath, he tipped the antique hurricane lamp from the nightstand over onto the bed, making sure that most of the kerosene inside it spilled over Chuck's head and hand. When they'd bought the house three years earlier, he hadn't wanted to furnish it with antiques, modern being more to his taste, but Bettyann had insisted. Now he was glad.

He stepped backwards, fists on his hips, trying to get the full effect. Yes, it would look very much as if the man on the bed had collapsed there feeling ill, lit a cigarette, fallen asleep, and rolled fitfully over onto his side and knocked the lamp over by accident. He nodded, pleased. He was certain no one would question it.

Still standing well away from the bed, he lit a cigarette, watching the Zippo's flame waver in the breeze between the bedroom window and the bathroom. Then he put the pack and lighter on the nightstand.

He took a few puffs, and then gingerly inserted the lighted Old Gold between the second and third fingers of Chuck's hand. He figured he had about ninety seconds until it burned down and ignited the kerosene.

Moving quickly through the house to the back door, he paused for a mere scintilla of time for one last look. It was a nice house, but working hard enough to pay for it had been killing him. He shrugged away any regrets; it would be a lot better this way.

He went outside to the garage, opened the door with the control mounted on the side wall, slipped behind the wheel of the old Roadmaster, and backed out. He wasn't worried about anyone seeing him, because the couple in the house on one side of his both worked; the widow on the other side also had a day job.

By the time he reached the corner, he could see black smoke snaking out the bedroom window at the side of the house.

He drove east, stopping for a moment in a supermarket parking lot where he deposited Chuck's duffel and the extra pills into a trash receptacle. Then he headed downtown, put his car in a parking garage adjoining one of the big hotels, and crossed the street to climb into a waiting cab. One nice thing about downtown, he thought, is that you could always get a taxi.

"Airport," he told the driver.

Once at the terminal, he went directly to the storage locker where he'd stashed a suitcase three days earlier. New suitcase, new clothes—just enough to get him through the first week in the little seaside town on Mexico's Baja Peninsula until he could buy some more with the twenty-one thousand dollars in cash, also in the suitcase, he'd amassed slowly by selling some stock shares over the past months.

He'd even filled out the luggage tag on the suitcase. "Michael Mitchum," it read, the same name as on his forged passport. Close enough to his own name that he wouldn't forget it, different enough that no one would make the connection.

Not that anyone would try. Meacham Donalson was by now burnt to an unrecognizable crisp in an unfortunate house fire. Poor fellow. His wife was in New York when it happened. She'll be devastated.

Just devastated enough to collect the two million dollars on his double indemnity policy, he thought, smiling, to collect more insurance money on the house, and to join him in Mexico in two months, maybe three, as they'd planned.

However long it took, it would be worth the wait to spend the rest of their lives in the sun with all the money they'd ever need. He briefly considered calling her at her sister's home in Larchmont, just outside New York City, to tell her that things were progressing on schedule, but thought better of it.

He removed four hundred dollars in cash from the suitcase and then checked it through to San Diego where he'd change planes for the short flight to Puerto Vallarta. The truth was, he would have preferred driving all the way, taking his time and seeing the sights along Route 66 like any other tourist, then turning south at Gallup and proceeding on to San Diego. But he knew the old Buick would never have survived the trip, and besides, there was something to be said for getting on with his new life and his new identity as quickly as possible.

With two hours before his flight was scheduled to leave, he went into the cocktail lounge at the terminal and ordered a Budweiser. It would be his last St. Louis beer, he thought; from now on he'd be drinking the Mexican stuff, Dos Equis or something. It would take some getting used to.

He glanced up at the TV set which was playing some witless game show, but he wasn't concentrating, thinking instead about how good it was going to be in Mexico—free from pressure and worry and responsibility, living in relative luxury with Bettyann for the rest of their lives.

It wasn't until halfway through his second Bud that he remembered something, and his face grew ashen as clammy sweat broke out all over his body. He began to shake, spilling some of his beer on the bar top.

The bartender came over to mop it up with a towel and noticed his customer seemed ill. "Hey, buddy, are you okay?" he said.

But Meacham Donalson couldn't answer, because there was a lump in his throat that felt like a basketball, and his stomach was knotted up inside by the harsh twist of fear.

By the time the Fire Department got the blaze contained, half the house was gone. The entire street was cordoned off, much to the dismay of the homeward-bound residents of that particular housing tract who often used it as a thoroughfare to get to their own homes two and three blocks over. The acrid smell of smoke hung in the air for a quarter mile in either direction, and closer to the house was another sweetish smell that few of the neighbors could identify but that the firemen and Detective Sergeant Harry Guska recognized as the scent of burnt flesh.

Guska stood on the front lawn, occasionally bringing a handkerchief soaked with old Spice aftershave up to his nose and mouth, talking with Fire Department Captain Henry Schreiber.

"There's not much left of the poor bastard," Schreiber was saying, his perspiring face speckled with soot. "Not much left of that side of the house, either. The open windows fed that fire pretty good."

"I wonder why the windows were open on such a hot day," Guska said, shaking his head to fight down the nausea that washed over him like a strong and persistent surf. As soon as the flames had been put out, he'd gone in to look at the body. He wished he hadn't. "You'd think he'd want air conditioning."

"Damn shame," the fireman said. "I met him a time or two—at Chamber of Commerce breakfasts. Not a bad guy. Pretty wife, too." He wiped sweat from his face, turning the specks of soot into long smudges. "Looks like he was smoking in bed, fell asleep and knocked the kerosene lamp over."

"Pretty dumb having a kerosene lamp in the bedroom anyway, wasn't it?"

"It was part of the décor," Schreiber said.

A dark Ford pulled up at the curb and the county coroner got out carrying his omnipresent black bag.

"I think he was on something," the fire captain continued.

"What do you mean?"

Schreiber shrugged. "There was what looked like a bottle of pills in the bedroom. Pretty burnt up, though."

Guska scribbled in his notebook. "I'll have my guys check it out."

A uniformed police officer came around the house and walked across the grass toward him. He had a handkerchief up to his nose, too, but Guska couldn't tell what it had been doused with.

"Got a minute, sergeant?" He made the word sound like "sarn't."

Guska nodded to Schreiber and followed the young cop up the driveway along the charred side of the house.

"I checked out the garage," the uniform was saying. "The guy's car was in there, all right. A big Caddy."

"So?"

The young cop's nose wrinkled. "Take a look for yourself."

They went into the garage. Since it was a good forty feet from the house it had sustained no damage, although its white paint was darkened by smoke.

The uniformed cop opened the right rear door and stood aside so Guska could see in. On the back seat was a large sheet of graying cardboard on which the words WILLING TO WORK had been hand-painted.

"What do you think of that, sergeant?"

Guska stood very still, looking at the sign. Then he leaned

into the car and lifted it out, holding it carefully by the edges so he'd leave no fingerprints.

"I don't know," he said, frowning hard. "But I'm sure as hell going to find out."

Amazingly enough, this is the very first, and so far only, short story to feature my Cleveland sleuth, Milan Jacovich, who has appeared in thirteen novels thus far. I don't know why I've kept him prisoner in the longer form. Perhaps I see him as a larger-than-life figure who needs a bigger canvas. But this story seemed to cry out for his tender ministrations.

It was inspired by actual events that took place in Cleveland in the summer of 1999. There was no murder, of course, but the background—the Ku Klux Klan rally, the embattled mayor fighting off the press and the city council, the enraged citizenry—is as true as I could write it without incurring a lawsuit.

When the story was first published I expected angry phone calls from the public figures I so casually disguised before savaging them, but to date there have been none.

I am pleased to report that in a city where the African American population is about sixty percent, the actual rally went off without a hitch; it was rather poorly attended, there was no violence, no national press coverage, and other than taking a deep bite out of Cleveland's annual budget, no harm was done. The Klan wasted its time, which pleased me very much.

The Gathering of the Klan

Just about the biggest controversy to hit Cleveland since the old Browns released Bernie Kosar in mid-season back in the early nineties was the announcement that our African American mayor had granted a permit for a rally outside the Cleveland Convention Center on a Sunday afternoon in August to an out-of-town contingent of the Ku Klux Klan.

Probably no one was as surprised as the klunks, klowns and kleagles themselves; their usual M.O. was to apply for a permit in some northern city, and then sue for the right to Free Speech when the permit was denied. They had accumulated quite a comfortable little nest egg from collecting such judgments in towns in Michigan, Pennsylvania and Minnesota over the last several years, and they were probably planning on collecting big from liberal and heavily black populated Cleveland.

Everyone was mad at the mayor. The police department's union, the African American community, the city council and the county commissioners, all of his many political enemies and rivals, and most of the media had taken the opportunity to try to shoot him down. Everyone was terrified that Cleveland would once again become a national laughing-stock, to say nothing of the genuine fear that one hastily-hurled racial slur or one thrown beer can could set off a riot that would see the city go up in flames.

The mayor pleaded that his hands were tied and talked a lot about the First Amendment, and begged the citizenry to behave itself and not give the national media any sound bites which with to tarnish the image that Cleveland had taken such pains to rebuild and polish over the past twenty years.

I try to stay out of politics; as the sole owner of a small business—Milan Security, which I christened after my own first name, Milan, since my surname is almost impossible for many people to pronounce—supplying industrial security and private investigations, I have enough to do just trying to keep solvent. My natural dislike and loathing for anyone promoting racial hatred made me follow the story closely in the newspapers, but I had no intention of getting involved in it one way or the other.

Until Earl Roy Ruttenberg, the regional president and exalted Grand Dragon of a southern Ohio branch of the Klan, walked into my office five days before the rally wanting to hire me as his personal bodyguard for the weekend of the rally.

He was close to fifty, some forty pounds overweight, slightly balding, and had a complexion like four-day-old cottage cheese. He came in flanked by two over-muscled young men who were twenty years younger; both had bad hair and Elvis sideburns and UP WITH WHITE PEOPLE T-shirts, and looked as though they were totally ignorant of even the whereabouts of the nearest dentist. One of them had a girlish, soulful look like Paul McCartney. Ruttenberg sat in one of my client's chairs, but his two trained orangutans positioned themselves on either side of the door.

I listened to his offer of a two-day job as his bodyguard and turned him down flat.

"I'm truly sorry to hear that, Mr. Jacovich," he said, his accent that blend of southern and midwestern that you hear down near the Kentucky-Ohio border and which is referred to as "briar," after the somewhat disdainful sobriquet, "briar hopper."

"Sorry," I said.

"I've asked around, believe me, gotten lots of recommendations, and you're definitely my first choice."

"I can't imagine why," I said. "First of all, I'm Catholic, and secondly I despise everything you stand for and I have nothing but contempt for the line of shit you're trying to sell."

Ruttenberg smiled easily. "A lot of people feel that way."

"Maybe you should go find a bodyguard that doesn't."

"You're not saying that you'd like to see me dead, are you?"

"I don't want to see anybody dead, Mr. Ruttenberg. But if the whole world was on the *Titanic* and I was in charge of the lifeboats, I don't think you'd get one of the first seats."

He laughed; he had a *yuk-yuk-yuk* kind of laugh that grated on my nerves almost as much as his racial attitudes. The T-shirt muscle boys guffawed too, but I don't believe they got the humor; they were programmed to laugh when the Grand Dragon did.

"You seem as if you're pretty well-protected already," I said.

"Oh, Ozzie and Jay are great for the everyday stuff. But I know that our being here on Sunday has caused a lot of controversy, and I was hoping to find someone who really was plugged in to Cleveland, who knew the crazies to look out for."

"From where I stand, it seems to me that the crazy we have to look out for is *you*."

"Ah-ha-ha," he said, but it wasn't a laugh this time. "I'm a crazy who's prepared to pay you very well, though."

"If I tried to spend your kind of money, Mr. Ruttenberg, I'm afraid I'd disappear in a puff of sulfurous smoke."

"You'd druther see some wild-eyed funky nigger with a razor cut my throat?"

I glanced out my office window at the Cuyahoga River, which ran past the building. As a big guy who used to play defensive tackle on the Kent State football team, I figured that with a good enough throw I could probably toss Ruttenberg into it with ease. "Say that word again in here, Mr. Ruttenberg, and you're going to have to swim home." The muscle guys stirred uneasily at the threat. "And the same goes for Ozzie and Harriet over there, too. Try me if you think I'm kidding." I fantasized the scenario for a few seconds and added, "Please try me." Hope springs eternal.

"I am truly sorry I offended you, Mr. Jacovich," Ruttenberg said. "It's just a word, after all."

"It's an ugly, hate-filled word that I never allow in my presence. I can't fault you for being stupid, because you probably can't help it. I can, however, blame you for being rude. Remember that. Or don't bother, you're leaving anyway."

"I think you owe me the courtesy of a hearing, at least."

"I don't owe bigots the sweat off my ass."

"Looky here," he said. "We're entitled to our b'liefs just like anyone else. And I can assure you that my people are completely under control and will cause no trouble at all unless they are physically provoked. *Physically* provoked, you understand. We've been called names by the best of them, that doesn't bother us."

"Then you won't have any trouble and you won't need me. Besides, this city is going to great expense to make sure nobody offs your sorry ass when you put on your clown costumes and wave the flag."

"They are that, and I appreciate it." He said the last word like Andy Griffith used to, without the first syllable. "It's the time leading up to the rally that has me worried.

"We don't want any riots. That'd run counter to our purposes. But d'you have any idea what might transpire here if anything happens to me? Or to *anyone?* Chaos," he intoned, pronouncing both the *C* and the *H* like he would if he were saying "chicken." He leaned back in the chair and crossed his legs. "People will get hurt, maybe innocent people, maybe some of your tippytoe-dancing liberal and black friends. You see the truth in that?"

I did, but I didn't tell him so.

"You want that happening here in your city? I don't b'lieve you do, do ya?"

Once again, I wouldn't give him the satisfaction of answering a question that was, after all, rhetorical.

"So here's the deal. The city of Cleveland is providing security at the rally, but before that, we on our own. Now, we're gonna check into our hotel on Sattidy afternoon. We want you there just to make sure there isn't any trouble. We eat dinner, you join us—dinner is on me, of course—and at nine o'clock we turn in. We're country people, we go to bed early. Sunday morning you meet us at the hotel, you escort us to the rally, and then the Cleveland po-lice take over and pertect us from those people who don't like what we have to say and wanna deny us our right to free speech under the first amendment of the constitution of the United States. You're free to leave then. You don't even have to stay and listen to the speeches." He gave me what he thought was a winning smile. "Although you really oughta, you might learn somethin'."

"I could learn the same things from the wall of a truck stop men's room."

His mean little eyes got even smaller; he didn't like that. He didn't like *me*. I could live with it.

He was a gamer, though, I had to grant him that. He didn't give up. "So you gonna he'p us out here? Or are you willin' to jus' sit back and maybe watch your home town burn?"

Now, I am not possessed of sufficient hubris to think that the safety of Cleveland's citizenry depended on me. But the son of a bitch did have a point. American cities today are as volatile as gasoline fumes, and it wouldn't take much of a spark at a public breast-beating where one group disses another in the ugliest of racial terms to set off a conflagration for which Cleveland would have to apologize for the next thirty years.

Maybe I could make a very small contribution toward keeping a spark from striking.

"All right, Mr. Ruttenberg, I'll do it. As long as we completely understand each other."

"What's there to understand?" Ruttenberg asked, taking a checkbook out of the breast pocket of his discount-store suit.

"That I despise everything about you," I said.

My pal at *The Plain Dealer*, Ed Stahl, whose column used to grace page two every morning but due to the paper's new format was now buried deep inside where nobody could find it, was frankly appalled. Over the past three weeks since the rally was announced, he had filed several scathing columns excoriating the Klan and the mayor for granting them access to public space, along with the mayor's political enemies who protested that he was coddling bigots and racists and were using the opportunity to savage him for their own aggrandizement, and just about everyone else in town, too. Ed had received several ugly and even threatening voice mails for his pains, most of them from gravel-voiced men who sounded, he said, like refugees from *Deliverance*.

"I think you're making a mistake, Milan," he told me over pasta at a table by the window in the front room of Piccolo Mondo on West Sixth Street. "Those people are pigs. You know what happens when you lie down with pigs."

"I do," I said. "But it seems preferable to a riot."

"That Earl Ruttenberg is bad paper."

"He's a fat clown, Ed. And the only people who will listen to his crap are the morons who think like he does in the first place. He's preaching to the choir."

"If that's true, Milan, you win. So why are you worried about rioting?"

"Because there's a hell of a lot of people in this town, of all colors, who think Ruttenberg and his people should be used as garden fertilizer. If rocks and bottles and bullets start flying there won't *be* any winners."

He gulped down a slug of his favorite poison, Jim Beam on the rocks, and grimaced. Ed has an ulcer, and has no business drinking anything stronger than buttermilk.

"Is the money enough that you can live with yourself afterwards?"

"I'll let you know Monday morning," I said.

He glanced up at the door and his shoulders grew rigid. "Oh my," he said. "Oh my fucking stars. . . ."

I followed his gaze. Entering the restaurant was one of the most familiar faces—and loudest voices—on the local scene. After a long tenure as de facto leader of Cleveland's African American community, Clifford Andrews had been elected to a lively and volatile mayorship for four years that were characterized by violent temper tantrums and black-power rhetoric, before losing City Hall in a close election seven years ago to the current two-term incumbent, a setback for which he had never forgiven his former friend, and had been not-so-subtly trying to undermine his successor ever since. Now forced into the private practice of law on Cleveland's largely black east side, Andrews had made enough political hay out of the issuance of the KKK permit to last the farmers of Kansas several lifetimes.

He bore down on us, eyes lasering into Ed Stahl, his cocoa-brown face glistening with perspiration, flanked by two very large black men one might be forgiven for mistaking as Cleveland Browns offensive linemen, and stopped at our table.

"Hello, Clifford," Ed said.

"Stahl, don't you hello-Clifford me, you race-baiting son of a bitch." Andrews was enough of a presence that most people look up when he enters a room, but the volume of his voice made sure that anyone who had missed his grand entrance at first corrected their oversight.

Ed just smiled up at him with the innocence of a Christmas-card cherub. "I'm glad to know you're still reading my column, Clifford. Although only you would call it race-baiting."

"You say I'm trying to start a riot in this city just to make myself look good? I ought to crack you across the face."

I shifted uneasily in my chair. Clifford Andrews was sixty-three years old and suffered from arthritis, but was not beyond the bar-fight stage, not by a long shot. During his administration he had been known to throw ashtrays, crockery, and on one occasion a folding chair at people who angered or disagreed with him. He also outweighed Ed Stahl by about eighty pounds.

"Clifford," Ed said, remarkably calm under the circumstances, "if I only wrote my column so that no one ever got their feelings hurt, I'd wind up selling ties at Dillard's. I think you acted irresponsibly, and whether you like it or not, it's my job to say so. Nothing personal."

"We'll see about that," Andrews said. Then he looked at me and his eyes blazed even more. "You're Jacovich, right?"

"Close enough, Mr. Andrews," I said. He had incorrectly pronounced the *J;* the correct way is YOCK-o-vitch. But I sensed Clifford Andrews didn't care one way or the other.

"I hear that you're the son of a bitch who's actually gonna protect those scum."

"Word gets around."

"How can you even look in the mirror?" he sneered. It was almost funny coming from him, the man who'd fanned media fever and street anger over the triple-K hate hoe-down from a warm coal to a white-hot ember.

Almost.

"I guess from time to time we all have trouble looking in mirrors, Mr. Andrews," I said.

His dark skin grew even darker as the blood rushed to his face. Then his lips tightened into a smile that could best be described as satanic. "You'll get what's coming to you, too. You and your honky racist employer, too. I'll see to it," he promised, and stalked off into the inner dining room. His two companions gave me a lingering look before they followed him.

Everybody else in Piccolo Mondo was giving *us* the looks. I just ignored them, but Ed boldly stared them down until they went back to their pizza and pasta.

"Move over, Ed. I guess I've just joined you on Clifford Andrews' shit list."

Ed laughed. "Welcome to the club. His shit list is longer than the one that tells who's naughty and nice." He took a carbon-crusted briar pipe out of his pocket and stuck the well-chewed stem between his teeth. No smoking was allowed in the dining room, but there was no law against pretending to. "I have to say that as mad as Clifford has ever been at me, he's never threatened me before, Milan."

"That bothered me, too," I said. "Well, look on the bright side—he didn't throw any furniture."

But Andrews did hurl a good bit of invective my way when he spoke to the Channel 12 news anchor, Vivian Truscott, on the six o'clock news that evening, calling me an even worse racist than Earl Ruttenberg who, in Andrews' words, "at least has the guts to be up-front about it." I've been called dirtier names, I suppose, although rarely with less justification, but I still had to hope that my two sons didn't hear it.

Those particular three of my allotted fifteen minutes of fame on the news show did prompt two unexpected office visits the next morning, one from a longtime business associate and the other from someone I had heard about but never met.

The business associate was Willard Dante, who ran the largest manufacturing company of residential and security devices in Ohio, in the not-too-close exurb of Twinsburg. He garnered national recognition a few years ago with his development of a stun belt that had civil libertarians picketing outside his factory, but my relationship with him was based more on the alarm systems, surveillance cameras and security paraphernalia which I purchased from him on occasion for my more paranoid industrial clients. He was the kind of church-tithing, flag-waving super-patriot I didn't have anything to do with socially, but our business dealings had always been cordial.

"I was on one of my rare trips downtown anyway today, Milan," he said heartily after I'd poured him a cup of coffee, "so I thought I'd pop in and tell you in person that I thought what Cliff Andrews said about you on TV last night really stinks the big stink. You deserve better."

I shook his outstretched hand. "Thanks, Will, I appreciate it. But I can't say it really bothered me. Andrews rants and raves all the time. Not that many people listen to him anyway."

"Well, I think you're doing the right thing. Somebody somewhere is going to blow Ruttenberg away for his sins one of these days, but I'd just as soon it didn't happen here. I'm glad you're on board to see it doesn't happen."

"The police are going to baby-sit him in public on Sunday," I said. "There's more security planned than if the pope was going to show up."

"I know," he said. "The mayor is breaking out the tear gas, and I heard a rumor there would be snipers up on the rooftops. Snipers, for God's sake. In *Ohio!* So what does Ruttenberg want *you* to do for him?"

"Make sure he and his Keystone Klunks check into their hotel with no problem, for one thing. And then I have to eat dinner with them. The next morning I drive him downtown to his slimefest, and then I'm through."

"I'd think that they would be staying at a downtown hotel, for the sake of convenience," Dante said.

"They're too cheap for that, Will. They've booked twenty-five rooms at a dinky little motel out by the airport."

"My stars," he said. He was the only person I'd ever met who said "my stars" as an exclamation and didn't sound like somebody's grandmother. "That's tacky. Where are you going to eat with them? McDonald's?"

"No, they picked this little low-end steak house close to their motel, a place called Red's, for God's sake. I think I'm going to eat before I go."

He laughed. "Anything I can do to help out? Want to rent some security cams?"

"I don't think we'll need them, Will."

He nodded, looking a little disappointed. "Well, listen, pal, I just wanted to let you know that I'm with you a hundred and ten per cent on this one, and that what old Windbag Andrews said about you last night is not going to affect our business relationship in the slightest."

"I appreciate the support, Will."

"What are friends for?" he said.

Well, it was nice to get an attaboy when the rest of the world seemed ready to hang me on the wall. A few of my friends had called me at home the previous evening to complain about Andrews' vilification of me on television, but no one had dropped in except Willard Dante. I had visited his Twinsburg plant several times, but I don't think he'd ever been in my office before.

About five minutes after he left, my second visitor arrived,

185

and I wondered if they had crossed paths in the parking lot. I'd seen him on television, seen his photo in the newspaper countless times, and had even heard him speak once when he made an unsuccessful run for the office of county commissioner a few years earlier. The Reverend Alvin Quest of the Mount Gilead Baptist Church on Cleveland's east side was a moral and spiritual leader in the black community, who had made a brief and spectacularly unsuccessful run for a U.S. Senate nomination a few years earlier. He was a consistent voice of reason and, when the occasion called for it, of fire.

In my office, however, he spoke with warmth and courtesy in a soft and well-modulated voice, his dark eyes sparkling behind his small, thick-lensed spectacles.

"It's a pleasure meeting you, Reverend Quest," I said. "I've been an admirer of yours."

He smiled. "Thank you," he said. "That's good to hear."

"So I hope you haven't come up here to give me a spanking about this Klan thing."

"Just the opposite," he assured me. "To be sure, Clifford Andrews and I share the same goals, but we usually differ sharply in how we want to accomplish them. I apologize for his rashness on the news last night."

"No harm, no foul."

"Actually I came here to offer you any help I can."

That one brought me up short. "Help?"

He nodded. "It would be very destructive to what our people have tried to accomplish in Cleveland if anything untoward were to happen to Mr. Ruttenberg or any of his minions. To say nothing of tarnishing the name of a city that has come so far in the last twenty years. So it is vitally important to me that Earl Ruttenberg stay safe as long as he is in our city. I'm more than happy to dispatch some of our people to help you with your security."

"You think that's such a good idea, Reverend? Letting the world see black men actually protecting the head of the KKK?"

"Oh, we'll be there having our say as well. The city of Cleveland has set aside a special area for protesters, just like they have for the Klan supporters. I'm sure you read that in the papers."

I nodded.

"But it will be a peaceful, quiet, dignified protest. I want to let everyone know that there are other avenues besides violence, that we defy those sad, silly, misguided fools in their sheets and hoods. That there is sanctity in human life, and that under the skin people are all the same. Isn't that what Martin Luther King preached?"

"Martin Luther King," I said, "never met Earl Roy Ruttenberg."

Not knowing, of course, that soon Dr. King was to have his chance.

It was Saturday afternoon and I was sitting in the so-called lobby of the Pine Rest Motel on Brookpark Road near the Cleveland Airport. I don't know why they had named it that; there wasn't a pine tree within ten miles, and if the lobby furniture was of the same quality as the beds in the rooms it wasn't very restful, either. It wasn't the kind of hot-pillow joint where hookers plied their trade in cubicle rooms and pushers passed dime bags down by the ice machine, but it wasn't exactly the Ritz Carlton, either.

I was wearing a .357 Magnum in a shoulder harness under my sports jacket, but nobody seemed to notice that. Maybe sitting in the lobby heeled was the Pine Rest's dress code.

For the past hour there had been a trickle of rough-looking

white males with one piece of luggage apiece checking in at the desk; a few of them gave me suspicious glances bordering on hostile, but I suppose when your main source of recreation is running around wearing sheets and hoods and foaming at the mouth about blacks and Jews and Catholics, suspicion and hostility are your daily portion.

Finally at a few minutes after four, a vintage Cadillac pulled up in front of the motel office. Earl Roy Ruttenberg got out of the back seat, and Ozzie and Jay exited from the front. I walked out of the lobby into the heat of August.

"I see you got here all right," I said to Ruttenberg. I made no effort to shake hands, nor was he expecting me to do so.

"So far, so good. Kind of a boring trip up from Medina, with all that highway construction. All quiet around here? Any suspicious-looking characters?"

"A bunch of them," I said, "but they're all with your group."

"Heh-heh," he said. "No, I was thinking of those folks of the Negro persuasion."

I assured him that no "folks of the Negro persuasion" were in evidence except the room maids, walked him in to the front desk, followed by Ozzie and Jay, who today were sporting mirrored sunglasses in a pathetic attempt at looking cool, macho and bad-ass, and watched while they checked in. It had been pre-arranged that the boys of bummer would share a room next to Ruttenberg's, which turned out to be a suite, a sitting room with a bedroom attached.

I sat on the sofa and watched him unpack. He had brought a brown suit, white shirt, and an ugly tie, which he put in the closet, extra socks and underwear and a pair of brown shoes that went in the dresser drawer, and a sports jacket, gray slacks and a bilious green polo shirt which he laid out on the bed. Then I watched in amazement as he lovingly unpacked and hung up his white robe and hood. It was almost funny.

Almost.

"Tell me," I said, "do you have those sheets laundered commercially, or does your wife wash and iron them for you?"

"Go ahead and have your fun, Mr. Jacovich," he said good-naturedly. This time he pronounced it correctly.

"Where did you learn the correct pronunciation of my name?"

"Oh, I heard that loud-mouthed boogie talking about you on television the other night."

I started to get up from the sofa, but he raised a hand like a traffic cop stopping a line of cars. "Take it easy, now. You just told me I couldn't use the N-word; you didn't say nothing about boogie."

I just sighed. When he's right, he's right.

From his briefcase he took several stacks of flyers and brochures of racial filth and put them on the table near the window. I avoided them the way I would a pile of rancid garbage.

He pulled a silver hip flask from his pocket and unscrewed the top. "Join me?"

"No thanks."

He laughed. "Fussy who you drink with, huh?"

"Something like that."

"Don't be that way. No reason we can't be friends, is there?"

"There are a thousand reasons. I'm here to see no one takes a shot at you or sticks a knife in your eye, and I'll do that to the best of my ability. If you were looking to hire a friend, you dialed the wrong number."

"Your loss," he said. He unscrewed the top of the flask, and took a long pull at it. "Aaaaahhh," he breathed in satisfaction. The smell that wafted across the room told me it was not very good bourbon.

"What do you get out of this, Mr. Ruttenberg?" I said, partly to make conversation and partly because I really wanted to know. "You have to be aware that here at the beginning of the twenty-first century, a vast majority of the people are either hating your guts or just laughing at you."

"Some folks do," he admitted. "Like you. But I think you'd be s'prised at how many folks are starting to think my way. *Our* way."

"That's why you travel with two bone-breakers and hired me as extra security, huh? Because everyone loves you."

"Of course not. Not the kikes or the spics or the pope-lickers. And certainly not the mud people."

"Damn," I said.

"What?"

"We're going to have to amend our little agreement, Mr. Ruttenberg, and put a moratorium on all the racial and ethnic slurs, or I'm not going to be able to keep from pounding the piss out of you."

"Just trying to get your goat, Jacovich. And I seem to have done a good job of it. Well, okay, I'll be good. But I can't guarantee what kind of words my friends might say at dinner tonight. You gonna pound the piss out of all of them?"

I didn't respond.

"But let me answer your question. What do I get out of it? The—um—*minorities* in this country are going to take over if we're not careful. The Jews have all the money and they control all the newspapers and television, the blacks have all the jobs, and the Catholics keep on grinding out new little Catholics like sausages to suck up our tax money in welfare. This country was founded by white men, settled by white men, built by white men, fought for and died for by white men.

What I get out of it is reminding the white people of this country of that fact so they don't let the US of A slip out from between their fingers. And to remind the *others* that there's a whole bunch of folks who just aren't about to let them take our birthright from us."

"I see," I said, feeling as if an elephant had just stepped on my chest. I'd heard this kind of foamy-mouthed crap before; all of us have. But I never looked at it across the same room before, and it was causing me difficulty in breathing.

"So what I get out of it," he went on, "is a US of A that I'll be proud to leave to my children and grandchildren."

I suppressed a shudder. The thought of Earl Roy Ruttenberg actually breeding and reproducing was an unsettling one.

I had brought a paperback along with me, figuring I'd rather read than have to talk to him, so I sat by the window, occasionally glancing up from the page and out into the parking lot to make sure no one was out there with a bazooka, while Ruttenberg went into the bedroom to make some phone calls. He emerged at a quarter to seven in the sports jacket and snot-green shirt, his lowly face glistening from a very recent shave.

"Le's eat!" he said, and actually rubbed his hands together.

Red's Steak House is for people who have arteries like fire hoses. Gnarly steaks, French fries, meat loaf, roast duck, pork loin, and anything else one might cook with grease were featured prominently on the menu. For those who don't eat red meat, there was fried perch. Other than the desserts, there was not much else. There is a lounge attached to the dining room, the kind of bar where ordering a frozen daiquiri is indicative of either seriously impaired judgment or a death wish.

The Klan had been relegated to what Red's laughingly called their banquet room, a private dining room with two long tables—each table was actually five tables pushed together—that seated sixteen people each. Ruttenberg ensconced himself at the head of one of them and indicated that I should sit next to him. But frankly, I didn't think I could eat a thing, despite Ruttenberg's generous offer to pay for my dinner. It was less the prospect of a heart attack on a plate that engendered a loss of appetite, frankly, than the company. I opted instead to stand at the door, just in case I had to earn my money, and unbuttoned my jacket in the event I had to draw my weapon quickly. Ruttenberg actually seemed a little hurt, but Ozzie and Jay flanked him and made him feel safe, so he didn't need me.

Most of the flint-eyed, slack-jawed men I'd seen checking into the Pine Rest had showed up, some of them tackily and gaudily dressed for the occasion. I guess they operated on the theory that you can't spew misanthropic hatred at the dinner table if you aren't gussied up for the part.

After everyone had enjoyed a pre-dinner cocktail or four, the first course was brought out. As befitting his exalted station in life, Ruttenberg was served first. It was soup, chicken noodle from the look of it, and for a while the only sound in the room was sucking and slurping, like standing next to a sewer grating after a heavy rain. Then, when the soup plates had been cleared away, Earl Roy Ruttenberg tapped on his water glass with a fork, waited until his followers had quieted down, and rose.

"My fellow patriots," he said when he had everyone's attention. "First off, I wanna thank y'all for being here. The camaraderie of white men is something special—warm and loving and strong in its devotion to a righteous cause. And I am reveling in that camaraderie right now."

Applause, heartfelt and enthusiastic. Nothing like a warm-and-fuzzy to fire up a lynch mob.

"Naturally we're hoping for a big turnout tomorrow," Ruttenberg went on. "But that really isn't important anymore. Because just by *being* here, we've won the game. The Nigro politicians who run this town are at one another's throats already, and we couldn't have asked for more help from the liberal news media than if we'd paid for it!"

"Hear! Hear!" somebody said.

"But I wanted to give each and every one of you my personal and sincere thanks. We are the last line of defense in the United States, and I am just damn proud of all of you for . . ."

He stopped, got a strange look on his face, and burped.

" 'Scuse me," he said. "I am proud of each and every . . ."

And then his face got very flushed, his eyes grew wide, and he bent over almost double from the waist and vomited down the front of his green shirt.

If you've ever given serious thought to putting rat poison in your basement, you would probably rethink it if you'd watched Earl Roy Ruttenberg die. It took him about seven minutes, and from his roars of agony, his writhing on the floor, his vomiting black bile, and the horrible contractions that sent his body into spasm every few seconds, it was not an easy seven minutes. Someone called the paramedics, but they arrived far too late.

The Klansmen were bumping into each other in panicked disarray, but they were muttering darkly about revenge and paybacks as well. It's apparently true that when you cut off the head of a snake, the rest of the body lives on.

Lieutenant Florence McHargue of the Cleveland P.D.'s Homicide Division arrived a few minutes after the paramedics. She was cranky because such a high-profile victim had dragged her away from her Saturday night, and even crankier because she was a black woman whose duty had thrown her among a rattled mob of Ku Kluxers. She had temporarily ordered them all out into the main dining room of Red's Steak House where they were milling around bumping shoulders like nervous steers in a slaughterhouse pen.

She wasn't exactly overjoyed to find me there, either. Lieutenant McHargue doesn't like me very much, but as far as I've been able to tell she isn't really fond of anyone.

"I heard on TV that you were going to hold Ruttenberg's hand," she said. "This serves you right." She looked down at the body, which had been hastily covered with a couple of tablecloths until the coroner's technicians could arrive. "Serves him right, too."

"And there are only about three hundred thousand people in Greater Cleveland with a motive, too. This should be a slam-dunk for you, Lieutenant."

"Let's start with slam-dunking *you*," she said. "Talk to me."

"I can start with Clifford Andrews. I suppose you know about him hanging me out to dry on television the other night. Did you also hear that he threatened both me and Ruttenberg publicly in Piccolo Mondo the other day?"

"Oh yes," she said. "That got back to me in a hurry."

"I'd think, then, that you'd start with slam-dunking *him*."

"I will, believe me. But the fact is that while in public Andrews is a fire-breathing race-baiter, privately he is a very logical, reasonable, and even charming man. Most of the time, anyway."

"When he's not throwing furniture."

"At his age, he's lucky he can still lift it, much less throw it."

"Nobody had a better motive," I reminded her. "It kills two birds with one stone. He rids the world of Earl Roy

Ruttenberg and he makes the mayor look like a doofus."

"The mayor does that himself without anyone's help," she observed dryly; the mayor and the police rank and file regarded each other the way the Albanians do the Serbians. "What else?"

"Not much," I said. "Ruttenberg was a little obsessed about his safety, but obviously just because he was paranoid it didn't mean someone wasn't after him. Hate has a way of blowing up in your hand."

"We're questioning all the kitchen help and the wait staff. Who knew the Ruttenberg crowd would be eating here?"

"I have no way of knowing who they told. I know I didn't tell anybody." Then the skin prickled on the back of my neck. "Except Willard Dante."

"The stun-gun guy?"

"That's the one. I happened to mention to him that the Kluxers were going to be having dinner here. But he's a Pat Buchanan conservative; why would he want to kill Ruttenberg?"

"Why indeed," she said, and jotted his name down in her notebook. "This town catches fire this afternoon and his phone will be ringing off the hook with people wanting security cameras and alarm systems and even stun guns to protect themselves from rioters. What made you tell him and no one else?"

I had to think about that for a while. "Because he asked."

"Uh-huh," McHargue said.

Willard Dante's house was in the elegant little village of Gates Mills. Apparently the stun-gun business was a lucrative one. He seemed surprised to see me on his doorstep, because I hadn't called first. From what I could see over his shoulder into the formal dining room, he and his wife were apparently hosting a dinner party for two other couples, a casual one because he was wearing white sailcloth slacks and a fuchsia polo shirt.

He looked shocked when I told him about Ruttenberg.

"But why come all the way out here to tell me?" he wanted to know. "I had nothing to do with him."

"Is there someplace we can talk?"

He looked nervously back at his guests. "Sure, in the garden room."

Which turned out to be a quaint little utility room that had been done up with white wicker furniture and trellises against the walls. It was a peaceful room, the kind of room one sits in when the pressures of business were great and the batteries needed a little peaceful re-charging.

"Will," I said after we were both sitting down, "why did you come to my office the other day?"

"I told you. I was in the neighborhood, and I thought what a lousy deal you'd gotten from Clifford Andrews, talking about you on TV like that, and I wanted to drop by and show you some support."

"Support because I needed it, or support because you thought Earl Ruttenberg was a patriot?"

His face flushed. "That's a shitty thing to say, Milan. Sure I'm a right-wing conservative, and sure I've lived in Cleveland all my life and my favorite color isn't black, but I'm no Kluxer. I thought Ruttenberg was pig shit, to tell you the truth."

"Enough to slip rat poison into his chicken soup?"

"You aren't serious!"

"You made a point of asking me where Ruttenberg was staying and where they were going to eat. Why would you want to know that?"

Out in the dining room, everyone laughed. They were

having a lot better time than their host. "I told you I dropped by for support and friendship," Dante said, "and that's true. But I also came to see if I could do a little business. Remember I asked you if you wanted hidden cams put up?"

"I remember," I said.

"So trying to turn a buck or two makes me a bad guy?"

"Not necessarily."

"It sure doesn't make me a murderer."

"Who else did you tell about Red's Steak House and the Pine Rest motel?"

"Nobody," he said. "Who the hell would I tell?" Then his eyes got big and round. "Oh, wait," he said. "In the parking lot outside your office. I just happened to mention it in passing. Reverend Quest. Was he coming to see you, Milan?"

Lieutenant McHargue wasn't glad to see me the next morning; she never is. And she was overwhelmed with work, trying to coordinate the police presence at the Klan rally for that afternoon. But I had after all cracked her case for her, and she couldn't be downright rude and toss me out of her office.

"Go figure," she grumped. "A man like Alvin Quest. God!"

"He made a full confession?"

She nodded. "He sent one of his people in to Red's Steak House and got him a job as a busboy—using a phony name, of course; that's how the rat poison got in the chicken soup. The kid is long gone from the city and Reverend Quest will go to the execution chamber before he'll tell us his name. Quest's lawyer will probably plead temporary insanity. He may have something at that. Find me twelve jurors in this town who are going to send Alvin Quest to death row." She took a deep breath. "Frankly I'm more pissed off at him for trying to incite a riot in my city than for ridding the world of garbage like Ruttenberg."

"It's the same scenario as Clifford Andrews," I said, "only Quest's was more dignified and with a little come-to-Jesus thrown in. Certainly Quest had every reason in the world to hate Earl Roy Ruttenberg and want him dead. And if things blow up this afternoon, the mayor is going to have a whole Western omelet on his face. And that would give Quest the wedge he needed to run for mayor himself."

"Well, the joke's on him, Jacovich, and you too. Because there isn't going to be any blow-up. We've got every cop who can drag his or her ass out of bed with riot gear and tear gas, ready to uphold the constitution and protect the rights of a bunch of mouth-breathers with pillowcases over their heads. Or we will have," she said pointedly, "if you get the hell out of my office and let me do my job."

"Good luck this afternoon."

"Are we going to see you at the rally?"

"And listen to that kind of filth? No thanks. I have better things to do with a summer Sunday afternoon."

"Like what?" she said.

"I was thinking about straightening out my sock drawer."

I didn't go near my sock drawer after all, but I did stay home and watch the Indians play the Oakland A's on television. Jim Thome didn't hit a dinger, but the Tribe won anyway.

I stayed around for the six o'clock news, though, and was delighted to hear that the Klan rally passed without incident that afternoon. Less than a hundred Klan supporters showed up, probably because the keynote speaker was in cold storage with a tag on his toe. About twice that many anti-Klan protesters linked arms and sang "We Shall Overcome." The biggest contingent of all was the press, and they had precious little to write about when it was all over. No incidents whatsoever, no sound bites for the networks to use to castigate poor old Cleveland, and when it was all done the mayor came out smelling like the Rose of Tralee.

I was damned proud of my city that day. Cleveland can be a tough town, but it's always, always fair.

Additional Copyright Information:

"Little Cat Feet," copyright © 1991 by Les Roberts. First published in *Cat Crimes*.

"Good Boys," copyright © 1992 by Les Roberts. First published in the *Cleveland Plain Dealer*, August 1992.

"Angel of Death," copyright © 1992 by Les Roberts. First published in *City Reports*, December 1993.

"The Scent of Spiced Oranges," copyright © 1992 by Les Roberts. First published in *Cat Crimes II*.

"The Fat Stamp," copyright © 1993 by Les Roberts. First published in *Elvis Rising*.

"The Pig Man," copyright © 1994 by Les Roberts. First published in *Deadly Allies II*.

"The Catnap," copyright © 1994 by Les Roberts. First published in *Feline and Famous*.

"The Brave Little Costume Designer," copyright © 1998 by Les Roberts. First published in *Once Upon a Crime*.

"Willing to Work," copyright © 1999 by Les Roberts. First published in *Murder on Route 66*.

"The Gathering of the Klan," copyright © 2000 by Les Roberts. First published in *The Shamus Game*.